DUPLICITY

PAMELA MURRAY

BLOODHOUND
— BOOKS —

ALSO BY PAMELA MURRAY

Murderland (The Manchester Murders Book 1)
Bloodline (The Manchester Murders Book 2)

For my friends
Heather, Christine, Anita and Lindsay

It is said that every story has two sides to it. We begin to read a book, and when it is finished, we have read it. Read and read: two words, both the same, but with very different meanings. If stories are like that, can people be too? Can everyone have two sides to them? Let's see...

Jonas Burke – *Devilled*

1

The pantry door is slightly ajar, but there is enough of a gap for you to see what is happening in the kitchen beyond. He tells you to wait in there and keep quiet, and you do as you are told.

You see him take the knife from the block on the worktop and hide it behind his back before he turns around and takes slow, silent steps towards the table. A man is sitting there, his back towards him, head down and reading the evening newspaper just as he does every night at the same time without fail. He has no inkling of what is about to happen. How can he? There is no reason for him to suspect.

The assailant makes no sound; nothing to give his presence away, so his approach is unnoticed. It has all been carefully planned, and is now being carefully executed. The cold steel knife suddenly appears from behind his back; the light shining down from the fluorescent ceiling light above catching the edge of the blade and making it twinkle, making it magical.

Then everything seems to happen in slow motion. You hold your breath in anticipation, watching with unblinking eyes as the blade is carefully and precisely positioned at exactly the point it will enter.

Cold and unfeeling, with nerves of steel to match the cold material *of the knife, he thrusts it in deep with such a force that it enters the back of the man's neck and out the other side, the tip of the blade emerging bloodied from just beneath his chin.*

It feels good going in; much easier than expected. Much smoother than expected.

You gasp and he looks over, knife still held tightly though it has served its purpose.

He puts a finger to his lips for you to keep quiet.

You have never seen so much blood before; it makes you feel sick, and you put a hand over your mouth to catch what may or may not come out.

The man at the table cries out in shock, a red shower of blood spluttering from his mouth. He attempts to turn around, tries to understand what is happening to him, tries to see who has done this to him, but the knife is held firm and prevents him. Then his head falls heavy against the table.

The assailant withdraws the knife and throws it onto the kitchen floor, then vanishes from the scene.

You wait in the pantry for what will come next.

L ike her father, and his father before him, Hannah
   Sanderson had chosen to enter the police force.
      They had warned her about all the male chauvin-
ism, but a bunch of men weren't going to put her off her chosen
career. *Sticks and stones, and all that,* she told herself. However,
when she eventually got there, it was worse than she could have
ever imagined. At that time, the division between men and
women was very much an issue, with the former considering the
latter to be far inferior on all counts. A lot of her male colleagues
did their best to make her life, and the lives of other female
members of the force, a living hell.

But once she'd gained promotion after promotion on her
own merit, and had risen up the ranks leaving a lot of her critics
behind in the lower ones, it felt to her as if they'd been handed
their well-deserved comeuppance. She'd made some good
friends over the years, but also suspected that she'd also left a
fair number of the misogynist set disgruntled.

For the past few years she'd been on a retirement count-
down, with an app on her phone working out her last day to the
precise second.

Then, at long last, the day arrived for Hannah to hand in her warrant card, hang up her police lanyard and enjoy her new-found freedom. Of course she would miss her former work colleagues and friends – the ones who hadn't tried to undermine her capabilities, that is. You couldn't work for an organisation the number of years she had and not miss the camaraderie when it all ended.

It had only been three weeks since she'd bid it and them a fond farewell and walked out of the main entrance for the very last time. Thinking back, it wasn't even a glamorous exit; the glorious sweep she'd had planned out in her mind just hadn't happened.

She had been weighed down by presents galore not-so-neatly packed into two large supermarket carrier bags she'd found crumpled up in the boot of the car. They were far too cumbersome for her to sweep elegantly out of the door even if she'd wanted to. 'Struggled' may have been a more apt description. But it was certainly a very welcome exit.

When her 'end of days', as she'd affectionately called it, finally arrived, and she'd taken the lanyard off her neck and left it at reception, she felt an overwhelming sense of relief. But, perhaps more importantly, she felt free from the daily grind of setting the alarm clock and adhering to the working week routine. She now had all the time in the world to do those things she'd been promising herself she would do when this day finally came.

Well, that was the theory anyway. Truth was, now that she had all this wonderful time on her hands to do everything on her to-do list, new priorities had come along, sneaked in and taken over. One of them being her new love of reading, and crime novels in particular.

And yes, she was being modern and trendy and reading them on the Kindle her daughter had bought her as a retirement present in the hope that she might, as she'd put it, 'expand her literary horizons'.

In her job as a detective inspector with Northumbria Police you would have thought that she'd had enough of crime and criminals over the years, but here she was reading fictional stories about them ... and, dare she say it, enjoying them.

Daughter Amy was a secondary school English literature teacher, and was passionate about books and reading. She had always been horrified by the lack of books in her mother's home. The closest her mother had come to having a personal library was a selection of glossy magazines, particularly home makeover ones, which she'd picked up from the local supermarket on food shopping trips. Most of them hadn't even been looked at.

Hannah presumed that Amy had got the whole literature thing from her father's side, as he'd always had his head in some book or another when he was alive. Both she and Fred had been looking forward to retirement together. They had had plans to travel to far-off places they'd only seen on TV or read about in travel brochures, but he'd sadly passed away five years ago, just two months short of his official retirement date.

He'd never smoked at all in his life, not even during his younger years when smoking was the 'in' thing, but he had developed lung cancer and had very quickly deteriorated following the initial diagnosis. Hannah was grateful that he'd been spared the years of pain and discomfort from the dreaded Big C. She knew that he would have hated to endure that, for her sake as well as his own, as the pain of watching her watching him as his body started to shut down would have been far too much for him to bear.

The consultant had said that he had most likely developed the cancer from years spent breathing in the second-hand smoke from work colleagues. Ironic, really, that those who had smoked since childhood had escaped yet he, who had never even put a cigarette up to his lips, had succumbed to the disease.

So, all the plans for their golden years together had been snatched from them and extinguished in such a cruel way, snuffed out as quickly as grinding a cigarette butt underfoot.

So Hannah was thankful that they had been blessed with a child. Daughter Amy had been her rock since Fred had died. Losing her father must have been as hard for her as it was for Hannah to lose her beloved husband. But despite that, Amy was always ready and willing to support her mother at a moment's notice.

One of the perks of freedom from the daily work routine meant that she now had more time to spend with her daughter and granddaughter Camille (or Millie as she was known to one and all). Nothing delighted her more than for them to all go out together. Today they were in town to see if they could get Millie an outfit for a wedding they'd all been invited to. The two grown-ups already had theirs, but were finding it difficult to come across something they all agreed on for the seven-year-old young lady. It seemed she was becoming very particular about what she wore.

'Oh Mum, look!' Amy suddenly came to a stop as they were walking to yet another children's clothes store. Surprised, Hannah walked straight into her daughter.

Hannah's eyes followed her daughter's straightened arm down to its pointing finger and then on to the bookstore across the road. In the middle window an assistant was setting up a table featuring a display of some twenty or thirty books. The printed sign beside it read, 'Come Meet the Author – this Saturday 11am to 2pm.'

But what caught and held Hannah's attention wasn't the sales assistant and the skilful way she was setting it all up. It was the life-sized cardboard cut-out figure that was staring straight at her. The man had his trademark brown fedora hat perched rakishly on his head, and a cream scarf draped around his neck.

Jonas Burke, the UK's number one crime writer, often compared to Stephen King because of all the horror and gore in his books and his very detailed and precise description of murders, was coming to sign copies of his new book *Devilled* this weekend.

Hannah decided right there and then that she had to be first in the queue. She liked his books; she'd started reading them about a year ago when they were recommended to her by a close friend. They were realistic and vivid and reminded her of her days on the force, and if that wasn't a good reason to read them then nothing was. Plus, she so loved to put herself in the detective's place and try to solve the crimes in the books well before the end. His new book had already been predicted to top the book charts in the coming weeks in pre-sales alone.

'That's made my day!' she exclaimed, one foot already stepping off the pavement to take a closer look. She was completely oblivious to a dangerously close oncoming double decker bus.

'Granny!' Millie squealed at the top of her voice.

The driver had his hand on the horn as soon as he saw what was happening but Amy managed to grab her mother's arm just in time. Even so, the driver, much to his annoyance, had to slam the bus's brakes on.

Hannah mouthed 'sorry' to him as the bus passed but was greeted with a less-than-polite hand gesture.

'You nearly got yourself run over,' Amy chastised her mother. She was thankful that Hannah hadn't seen what the driver had just gesticulated. But it appeared that all her mother could see was the display in the window.

'Oh, stop exaggerating!' Hannah retorted, but this time she checked the road before stepping out onto it again. She didn't want her daughter to grab her arm and haul her back for a second time. Even if she was now officially in her golden years she didn't want Amy, or anybody else for that matter, to think that she had lost the plot ... but she simply had to get over that road.

When she finally reached the bookstore she stood completely still gazing at the standee in the window.

'Mum, I'm worried about you!' Amy laughed, shaking her head at her seemingly star-struck parent. 'Your pupils are actually dilated! Drooling over a famous personality at your age is just ... well, it just isn't right!'

However, Hannah wasn't going to let her daughter reproach her again. So she had an answer ready for her, and retorted triumphantly, 'Well you did say you wanted me to read more!'

Saturday morning, and Hannah felt as nervous as a young girl on her first proper date. She had spent an inordinate amount of time choosing her outfit and getting herself ready. Amy had said that she'd go with her and drive them both into town. 'Just to make sure you arrive safely, Mum,' she said. 'Another bus incident would be unacceptable.'

After parking up in the multi-storey car park, they walked directly to the bookstore through the shopping centre. Amy had to smile to herself as her mother stormed on ahead of her, such was her desperation to see this author! She was going at a pace which even exceeded Amy's own naturally quick one. She had not seen her mother move so quickly in a very long time.

They arrived at least twenty minutes ahead of the scheduled book-signing, but there was still a queue of people waiting to get in ahead of them. Hannah was upset that she hadn't been first in the queue; other like-minded individuals had beaten her to that enviable position, but at least she was fifth in line to meet the great man.

Jonas Burke attracted a wide age range of fans it seemed; young and old patiently lined up in a queue which had now reached the front of the store and went out into the street. They'd been right to arrive early. Hannah watched as those in front of her had a book signed for them in turn, and saw their faces as they left the table after the briefest of conversations with the 'master of suspense'. She envied them, but it would soon be her turn to be in front of the maestro, and she could feel her heart pounding in her chest like a drum the nearer she got to the table. Fourth ... third ... second ... and then it was her turn. She managed to successfully suppress a squeal of delight, which would have been highly inappropriate for a woman of her age.

'Hello, my dear,' Jonas Burke said to her. He actually *spoke* to her; the man *spoke* to her! Hannah thought that her knees would buckle beneath her, causing her to fall to the floor in an embarrassing heap in front of him ... and her daughter.

'Oh Mr Burke I'm such a fan!' she exclaimed. She scolded herself the instant she said it, but the words just seemed to flow out of her mouth of their own accord. How many times must he have heard that sentence? And here she was repeating it again like some over-enthusiastic parrot performing for its owner. How had she become such a fan-girl at her age?

He laughed. Not a put-on laugh but one which seemed to be the genuine sound of amusement. 'Please, call me Jonas!' he told her, opening the copy of the book in front of him. 'And to whom should I make it out?' Pen poised over the title page. His eyes caught hers, and for that brief moment she couldn't for the life of her remember who she was until Amy nudged her on the elbow.

'It's Hannah,' she spluttered, casting a sideways look of mock-disgust at her daughter. Amy rolled her eyes in despair whilst at the same time wondering why parents seem to become so embarrassing once they'd reached 'that certain age'.

Turning back, Hannah thought she saw a very brief hesitancy before he signed it and handed it over to her. The title jumped out of the page at her: *Devilled*, sharp black writing on a background of red and orange flames.

'Is it about the dark arts or about cooking?' she asked in all seriousness as she scrutinised the eye-catching cover.

At first Burke looked astonished, but then he put his head back and roared with laughter. Hannah couldn't understand what was so funny about what she'd asked. It seemed to her a natural observation.

'You're the first person to ask me that,' he said when he'd finally composed himself. 'Very astute of you, my dear.'

'Well, my mother is a retired detective inspector,' Amy chirped up proudly.

'Is that so?' Burke asked, suddenly taking a little more interest. 'Well in that case,' he continued, 'you will have to read the book to find out.'

They then seemed to stare at one another for more than decently acceptable.

Amy decided that this was the opportune moment to leave the store before they decided to take this mutual appreciation further. Besides, the queue behind them wasn't getting any smaller and each person in it was eagerly wanting their chance to come face-to-face with their hero. As much as she apparently would have liked it to be, this wasn't a meet and greet exclusively for her doting parent.

'Come along, Mother,' she said, taking hold of Hannah's arm. 'Mr Burke here has more people to meet and I'm sure that you don't want to take up too much of his time, now do you? Isn't that right?' The last question was aimed at the author, but he was still eye-locked with her mother.

'Yes, yes of course,' Hannah suddenly came out of her trance and smiled at Burke.

'Enjoy the book,' he said as she was walking away. But Hannah thought that she saw something in his eyes that she couldn't explain and, even more confusingly, something inside her which she couldn't explain. A memory, a ... what? What was it she was sensing?

'You know, he looks very familiar somehow,' Hannah said to Amy as they were leaving the shop.

'Well of course he does,' her daughter chuckled at the nonsense of that statement, 'he's a very popular author, isn't he? His face is well-known all across the globe!'

'Yes, that's probably it.' Hannah felt she could do no other than agree, yet there was still something about him that she couldn't quite put her finger on.

3

You wait and watch as the flashing blue lights pull up at the rear of the house, wondering if the same is happening at the front. You hope there are lots of police cars, and reporters too. More publicity! The neighbours will be out in force, crowding around to see what is happening in the hope of glimpsing something horribly gruesome. Isn't that what grown-ups are like?

The man's wife finds him, head slumped down on the table when she comes home from work. She calls the police; but not before you watch her reaction to the scene, taking in every move and every word she utters to the corpse in front of her.

She tries to lift him, to shake him, to wake him as she thinks he is asleep.

You hear her say. 'You promised you'd have my tea ready and waiting! Where is it? I've been out all day slaving and you've fallen asleep! How dare you.' But then she realises that his body feels cold, too cold. She hasn't seen the blood on the floor beneath him, or the knife lying beside the door. She lifts him up by his shoulders, then she lets go of him in shock, and his face slams back down again on the table. You hear a crunching sound as his skull makes contact.

The scream from her mouth echoes around the quiet room. It is ear-piercing.

The back door has been left ajar; a glass panel next to the handle has been smashed and a stone is lying on the floor below it. Anyone who comes to investigate will think it was a break-in.

It must be about ten minutes after her frantic 999 call that she ushers two plain-clothed police officers into the kitchen, accompanied by a young girl dressed in full uniform. A trainee constable, or a new recruit perhaps, but most certainly someone who has not come across such a crime scene like this one before. She looks so young, not that much older than you. She looks so pale. All the normal colour has completely drained from her face as she casts her eyes over the scene.

You watch as she retches, yellowy-orange lumpy sick spewing from her mouth and cascading onto the floor.

'Johnson!' One of the two officers shouts at her, 'Look what you've done. You've only gone and contaminated the crime scene now!'

'It's Johnstone, sir,' she manages to say as she rubs a hand across her mouth to rub the remnants of sick away.

He stares at her in anger and a raised vein throbs on his forehead. He isn't happy with her retort.

You watch from the cupboard. Silly girl, throwing up like that. What a weakling! Girls are so different to boys; they can't handle it. Then you think it is time to make your presence known, and you make a sound to catch their attention.

'What was that?' the tall officer who hadn't shouted at the girl asks. He moves towards the hiding place. Pulling open the door he finds you curled up in a ball on the floor.

Your mother screams, 'I didn't know anyone was in there. I thought he was out with friends.' The sentence trails off as she runs towards the pantry, but the second officer holds his arm across her body to stop her.

'Johnson, are you cleaned up?' the one in charge shouts through to the next room where he's sent the young girl. He still gets her name wrong.

A shaky voice calls back. 'Yes.'

'Well, get back in here and do your job then!'

You watch as she sheepishly returns, embarrassed by the vomit stains on her uniform. She looks to her senior officer for guidance, and he points over towards the pantry. 'You're a woman aren't you? Get over there and take care of that boy. Take him to one of the ambulance people and get them to take a look at him.'

The girl does as she is told. She knows that she has do what a senior officer tells her to. Your mother follows.

'Goodness knows what he must have seen,' the lead officer says to his partner. 'Must have been terrified to be huddled up like that.'

'Will we have to question him?'

'In time, but not now. We'll give him some space for now. There'll be plenty of time to speak to him later, away from all this.'

4

Eager to start reading as soon as possible, Hannah spent most of Saturday evening and Sunday morning with her head in her book. Occasionally, she looked at the title page and the words Jonas Burke had written to her. It read: 'To Hannah, my greatest fan'. Perhaps not entirely true as she'd only just been introduced to his work in the past couple of years. There must be more devoted fans out there, ones who had been with him from the beginning of his literary journey which she knew had started almost twenty years previously. She was a mere novice by comparison. She'd enjoyed what she'd read so far, but two pages into chapter eighteen, a chill went down her spine.

That can't be right, she thought to herself, reading the passage over again and trying to take it all in. Burke was describing in great detail the death of one of the characters, but that death brought with it a memory from her past which was far too personal.

It was something only she had known about, so how could the author know every last detail about it? Unless, of course, he had been made aware of it by someone else; someone at the scene, perhaps, or, heaven forbid, the official report had been leaked. The manner of death was the one feature of the case that had not been made public. It had not even been released to the family, and that was what disturbed her greatly. The police officer still in her was telling her that something was very off here. This was something she had to pursue.

She knew exactly who she needed to talk to.

Detective Sergeant Sally Fielding looked out of the conservatory in her mother's house in Boldon. It was early November but the bright morning sun shone directly onto where she was sitting. She loved being in there, and it had become her favourite room since coming to stay. It felt warm and relaxing, and she let her head fall back onto the sofa cushion and closed her eyes.

After the events of the past few weeks this was the respite she so desperately needed. She was on temporary sick leave. She could hardly use her official title to describe her current status. So today, and for the next few days at least, she was simply Sally Fielding, civilian. It had been a full week since she had been released from the hospital in Manchester following her run-in with a deranged serial killer. She had agreed to spend at least another couple of weeks on sick leave with her mother. Her sister Amanda said that she would also be popping in from time to time to see how she was. The reconciliation with her estranged family had been unexpected and she had her partner Joe Burton to thank for that one.

The reconciliation had always been at the back of her mind, but after thirteen years without contact she assumed that neither her mother nor her sister, or herself come to that, wished to reignite their relationship. But it appeared that a close encounter with death was something that reunited families.

She had been watching a film on her laptop when she heard the doorbell. She knew that it wouldn't be for her: nobody from her past life in the north east even knew she was back here, and even if they did why would they want to see her again after all this time? So, it had to be someone for her mother, or perhaps a cold caller.

She heard voices in the adjacent room: another female voice of the same timbre as her mother's. *One of her old friends*, Sally thought, and continued to watch the film without giving it another thought. However, before too long the patio doors opened and her mother came through them.

'Alice, dear,' she began.

'Mum, I keep telling you it's Sally now,' her daughter light-heartedly corrected her. She'd lived with her middle name as her first for over thirteen years now: all her colleagues at Greater Manchester Police knew her by that name and that was how she wanted it to stay.

'Sorry, I keep forgetting,' her mother apologised, 'but there's someone here who would like to have a word with you.'

Sally looked up questioningly. Who possibly knew she was here, apart from her co-workers in Manchester?

'I don't know if you remember Hannah Sanderson?' her mother continued, seeing her daughter's frowned expression, 'but she used to work with your father before ... well, before he died.'

Sally vaguely remembered her dad's partner. As she recalled, he was DS to her DI, and she had probably been the last person to see him alive. A nice, kindly woman as she recalled.

'Yes, I do actually. I think she's been to the house a few times, hasn't she?'

Mrs Fielding nodded. She was delighted to hear her daughter talk about the house in a familiar way. She was glad that she and her two daughters had been reunited with one another again after all this time. 'Come on through,' she said, 'I'll make us all a nice cup of tea.'

Sally followed her mother into the living room. Hannah Sanderson hadn't really changed a great deal. Perhaps the hair was shorter and whiter but, essentially, she looked pretty much the same as Sally remembered her.

'It's lovely to see you again,' Hannah said, holding out her hand.

Sally shook it. 'And you.' She returned the compliment, although slightly puzzled that DI Sanderson specifically wished to talk to her.

Hannah looked furtively towards the door Mrs Fielding had gone through to make the tea. 'This is a bit delicate,' she said, 'and I don't really want your mother to hear what I have to say to you.'

'Oh?' Sally's interest was immediately sparked. 'Okay, we could go into the conservatory if you wish?'

She had no idea what this woman was so desperate to say to her, especially out of her mother's earshot, but the secretiveness alone was enough for Sally to want to hear her out. She might be temporarily out of action but her police instincts certainly weren't.

'Yes, that might be a good idea,' Hannah said and followed the younger woman into the conservatory, sitting down on the chair indicated to her. Again, she looked over her shoulder towards the door then back to her companion.

Hannah had deliberated how she should approach the subject matter and decided that the direct approach had to be the best. From all accounts Sally Fielding was, like she had been, a dedicated police officer and would doubtlessly appreciate someone coming out and stating the facts. 'It's about your father,' she said.

Sally was taken aback, and her expression couldn't hide it.

'I'm so sorry,' Hannah said, seeing the shock on the girl's face. She got up from her seat and sat down beside her on the sofa, putting both her hands over Sally's clasped ones. 'The last thing I wanted to do was to come here and bring all this up again, but I felt that I had no option ... under the circumstances.'

Although stunned, Sally found her voice once again. 'What circumstances? What could possibly have happened that would bring up my father's name, and his death, again?'

Right then they heard Sally's mother approaching; the cups on the tray she was carrying were clattering against their saucers heralding her arrival better than any group of trumpeters could have done. Any guests to Mrs Fielding's house would be presented with proper china cups with matching saucers, a sugar bowl, and milk jug, together with a plateful of biscuits positioned neatly on a paper doily – and not just the cheap biscuits either, only the best from M & S was good enough for Mrs Fielding's visitors. Putting the tray down on the glass-topped rattan table, she sat on the single chair just recently vacated by Hannah.

Sally didn't quite know what to say to her, especially as she knew Hannah wished to speak to her on her own, but it was Hannah herself who made the situation less awkward.

'That's lovely, Mrs Fielding,' she began, 'and I hope you don't think that I'm being rude, but what I have to say to Sally is official police business and I really don't want to bore you with it all. Do you think you could give us just a few minutes on our own? I promise I'll let you know when it's over and we can all enjoy the lovely tea and biscuits you've brought us.'

Mrs Fielding took it very well, considering that it was her own house and Hannah Sanderson had in effect asked her to leave the room while the two of them talked. 'Why, yes,' she said, getting up as quickly as she had sat down. 'I'll just be in the next room.'

Hannah waited until she'd closed the door behind her before continuing. 'What do you know about your father's death?'

'All I know is that he had a heart attack while he was at work,' Sally said, but then her eyebrows furrowed. 'What exactly is it that you're trying to tell me?'

Hannah exhaled a long breath. She knew that this would happen one day, that she would be sitting down with one or more of William Fielding's family members telling them what exactly happened that fateful day all those years ago. 'This would never have come to light had it not been for something I've just read in a book.'

'I don't understand,' Sally reiterated. 'Are you saying that my father didn't die of a heart attack?'

'No, he did, but it was the circumstances surrounding his death that weren't fully disclosed to you and your family.'

Sally couldn't quite believe what she was hearing. All these years she, her mother and her sister had been led to believe that William Fielding had simply gone out to work one day and died whilst on duty. As no finer details had been forthcoming from anyone on the force it was assumed that he had succumbed whilst at his desk or, at the very worst, whilst out of the office in the car with his partner. All the family were far too shocked to actually ask for the small print at the time as she recalled, as the news was bad enough without going into all of that. But if that wasn't the case, what had actually happened to him then?

'Have you heard of the author Jonas Burke?' Hannah asked.

'Yes, I have heard of him,' Sally told her, now wondering where all of this was going.

'I started reading his books just before I retired,' Hannah continued, 'as they were recommended by one of my old work colleagues, and I have to admit I got into them. Even just got to meet him at a bookstore in Newcastle. But forgive me, I digress. I was reading the latest one, *Devilled*, and then I came to the part in chapter eighteen where he describes the murder of one of the characters. I was reading it and I just couldn't believe what I was reading.'

'Go on,' Sally said, becoming more and more intrigued by what Hannah was telling her. She cast a sideways look through the doors back into the living room. Her mother was sitting in front of the television with the remote in her hand going through the programme planner trying to find something to her liking. Sally thought it to be the best place for her.

'He described the manner in which your father died in very precise detail. It was as if he'd been there at the scene.'

5

Sally felt as if her whole world had just been turned upside down. She was at a loss as to what to say, and found it difficult to take it all in.

'Are you okay, my dear?' Hannah's soft voice brought her out of her thoughts. Sally wanted to say that she wasn't – for how could she be after that little revelation, but she just nodded. She wanted to hear more; she needed to hear more, to find out exactly what had happened that mournful day.

'We'd been on the trail of a killer, a serial one as it turned out,' Hannah began. 'We had no idea who he was but we'd had tip-offs and followed a good lead and found ourselves late one night in the grounds of a hotel in Boldon Business Park. Your dad went in first; he was always the first in, couldn't hold him back, ever.' She stopped for a few moments.

Sally couldn't decide if she was reliving the event or trying to suppress the memory of it and realised the retired detective was gathering her composure. 'I heard him cry out from the hotel's leisure complex, but by the time I got to him he was already lying dead beside the pool. What wasn't commonly known was that he had been tasered, and the device was left beside him. It was mentioned in the official report, but that's the thing, you see.

'The murder scene in Jonas Burke's new book is almost a carbon copy of the scene that day right down to the location being the swimming pool in a hotel. In the book, after the killer disposes of his victim in one of the hotel rooms, he is almost caught, but manages to evade capture by using a Taser on one of the detective team before the other arrives on the scene. It's as if he's describing the events of that day; he even says that the killer hadn't intended for the police officer to die, but that he'd had a heart attack due to the effects of the Taser.

'Burke even adds that your father called out to me. As a matter of fact, that's puzzled me to this very day – I have no idea what he called out, but it's the fact that Burke adds it to the story that bothers me.

'There hasn't been a day when I haven't gone over it in my mind, trying to work out exactly what he could have said. But the answer to that one has always eluded me. I think that he must have recognised the killer. There was only one person who had known what it meant, and he was unable to tell me. The answer to that riddle had died that day along with your father.'

'But how can that even be?' Sally was still reeling from all this.

'Jonas Burke has either got a very good researcher, who is somehow managing to gain access to restricted police files, or...'

'Or?'

'He's somehow heard about it from the person who was there, or it has been passed on by word of mouth.'

'But it was fifteen years ago. Why put it into a book now?'

'Time, I guess. Leave it long enough and the case won't be fresh in the mind.' Hannah's explanation held water, but the implications were astounding. 'I just happened across it by chance.'

'Let me think about this,' Sally said getting up. 'Can we talk further about it, away from my mother's house perhaps? Would tomorrow be okay, if you're free that is?'

'Yes, of course, that would be fine. I'm free every day now that I'm retired. Why don't we meet at ten thirty for coffee in Starbucks at the cinema, it's quite a nice little spot and I'm often there with my granddaughter. Do you know where that is, as I know that you've been away for a while?'

'Yes, I do as a matter of fact, I passed it recently when I was up here with work. Changed a bit from how I remembered it.'

'That it has,' Hannah agreed, adding, 'I'm sorry to have to bring this to your door, but I thought that it was something that you needed to know.'

'I'm grateful that you've told me.' Despite the gravity of it Sally really was grateful, and she also knew the implications. This was something that needed looking into. 'Let's get Mum back in here and have some tea. I don't know what she must be thinking.'

Hannah stood to call Mrs Fielding back in.

'Oh, and let's not upset her with this for the time being.'

'No, of course not.'

'There's another question that springs to mind, of course,' Sally added, more to herself than her companion.

'And that is?'

'How many other real murder cases are featured in Jonas Burke's books?'

All three sat and chatted while Hannah finished her tea and ate the two biscuits she'd selected from the plate. Her revelation had certainly given Sally something to think about.

Later, after Hannah had left, her mother hadn't asked what

she and Hannah had discussed. Being married to a police officer all those years had implanted a 'don't ask' philosophy into her. She knew not to question. If the need arose, she was sure that her daughter would talk to her about it. However, she did notice her daughter was more subdued. Whatever they had discussed, it seemed to have had a profound effect upon her.

For Sally, having to relive the memory of her father's death brought all the pain and heartache back home to her again. It had been a terrible time for the entire family: her mother had lost her beloved husband, and she and her sister had lost their precious dad. All this at the tender age of sixteen. But it hadn't changed her decision to join the police force, even though her mother kept telling her about the long hours her father had had to work. She believed it was the long hours that had led to him having a heart attack.

None of them had known what actually happened that day. Sally was shocked by that. Why hadn't they been told?

She knew that this was something she had to investigate, and it had sparked her into action. The only problem was she was currently on sick leave, and to start an unofficial investigation on something which was personal to her would certainly be frowned upon if Greater Manchester Police became aware of it. So, the only logical answer was to make them aware of it, as withholding anything just wasn't in her nature. But this wasn't just a case of her looking into the circumstances surrounding her own father's death, there was also the matter of how Jonas Burke the author came to know about it in such precise detail in the first place.

This warranted investigation by the police. She'd need to get help, and hopefully backing, from her employer to access the files. There was only one answer: to get in touch with her boss, DCI Ambleton, so she picked up her phone and rang, despite it being a Sunday.

'That's a very unusual request,' Ambleton said, after hearing her DS out. The pause while she considered what she'd just heard lasted a good two minutes, and Sally was on edge waiting for the response. 'Normally I would have to say no, as personal investigations are very much frowned upon not only by Greater Manchester Police but any other force in the country. But I'm putting myself in your position and trying to see it from your perspective so I am going to say yes to your request. Your father was a police officer, so this is personal to all serving members of the force, and retired ones too if it comes to that. If official police files are being accessed for the purpose of fiction then I feel that that, too, warrants further investigation. I'll back you all the way with this, Sally, and anything you want from me, please just ask for it.'

Sally breathed a sigh of relief.

'How are you feeling, by the way?' the DCI added.

Sally guessed her boss had heard the expelled air she thought was only audible to herself. But she appreciated the DCI asking about her health. 'I'm much better thanks, but the truth is now that I'm feeling that way, I'm just twiddling my thumbs and watching films all day long. Not that I'm minding that, but this little bombshell has spurred me into action.'

'I agree, but it can't be bad watching films all day!' Perhaps Ambleton was looking forward to the not-too-distant future when she could spend all day at home watching daytime television or films with her feet up on the sofa. It wasn't that far off now, as Sally calculated, perhaps eighteen months at most?

'But now that the seed has been planted,' Ambleton continued, 'I can understand your eagerness to pursue to discover the truth. I'm sure I'd want to as well in your position.'

6

'You might as well take my car,' Sally's mother told her the next morning, and she happily accepted the offer. She could have walked to her meeting with Hannah Sanderson if she'd felt active enough but she opted for the easy way out on this occasion.

'Now can you remember where you are going?' Mrs Fielding asked as she handed her daughter the keys to the Audi.

Sally felt as if she were a youngster again, being given money to pop down to the shops to pick up a loaf of bread or a bottle of milk. She laughed to herself, or so she thought, but she had inadvertently done it out loud.

'What?' her mother asked, laughing herself. 'You've been away for quite a while, you know, and things have changed a bit in that time.'

'I know, I know,' Sally reached out and took her mother's hands, which surprised Mrs Fielding. 'I'm 99.9 per cent sure that I know where I am going. Are those good enough odds for you?'

'Yes, those odds are good enough for me!'

'Okay then, I'll see you later,' Sally told her as she headed out of the front door, about fifty per cent sure of which direction to go in.

When everything had been finalised the previous evening with DCI Ambleton, Sally Fielding formulated her plan of action. She thought Hannah Sanderson's input would be invaluable. So when they had sat down with their coffees beside the large window of the café in the cinema complex, she asked Hannah if she would like to come in on the case with her.

In some ways Sally felt a bit like a traitor even sitting in a Starbucks as she was a hard core Costa girl at heart. However, their large cappuccino was enormous by comparison to her usual one back in Manchester, and she liked the selection of toppings on offer. She made a mental note to inform Joe Burton of the delights of Starbucks on her return to duty in Manchester. For such a down-to-earth man he didn't half like his fancy coffees!

Hannah, in turn, was thrilled that she'd been asked to play a part in all this. Sally's father had been her partner for more years than she cared to think about and he'd had her back on more than one occasion during that time, so it seemed only right that she should do her bit to help get him the justice he deserved. She had hoped that she'd be asked, but hadn't dared to expect it.

'Let's just call you a consulting detective then,' Sally told her after Hannah had accepted her proposition.

Hannah laughed. 'That makes me sound a bit like Sherlock Holmes!'

'But without the deerstalker hat,' Sally retorted.

'I'd heard that you're a big movie fan.' Hannah thought to change direction and make the conversation more casual now that she had been asked to join the investigation. It would also be a good chance to get to know her former partner's daughter a little bit better.

'That I am,' Sally confirmed.

'Favourite actor?'

Sally smiled to herself. She did have a favourite actor and, as a matter of fact, was watching him on her laptop only yesterday when Hannah had called to see her. Her partner Joe was well aware of her inexplicable passion for the man, (in his eyes, certainly not in hers), and on more than one occasion had referred to him as her 'Mr Right'. She wished!

'I do,' she said, in answer to Hannah's question, 'but that's for me know and for nobody else to find out!'

'Very wise, my dear,' Hannah chuckled, remembering back to her youth when she'd developed strong feelings for a young boy in her class. One of his friends had found out and told him, and, embarrassed beyond belief, she'd stayed off school for a week until she could bear to face both him and his friends again.

That morning Sally had contacted DCI Paul Winters at Northumbria Police. He'd been helpful and approachable when they'd met recently and, as she'd just recently discovered, Hannah actually knew the man as they'd worked together in the past. So, there again, another strange link in this very odd case. Thankfully she had retained his contact details.

'Ah, yes, I've been expecting your call, DS Fielding,' DCI Winters said when Sally had called him.

'Oh?' she asked, taken aback.

'I've just had a call from DCI Ambleton; she thought it appropriate to inform me about the upcoming investigation.'

'Ah, I see,' Fielding said. She should have expected it really as Ambleton and Winters had been in touch with one another during the previous case, but she was so tied up with the prospect of investigating her father's death that she had momentarily overlooked inter-force diplomacy – and the investigation hadn't even started yet.

Then his tone became a little more serious. 'I was very upset to hear of your ordeal since the last time we met.'

She thanked him for his concern, but felt disinclined to discuss it further; she now had a new mission, and that was to find out the truth behind her father's untimely demise.

'So, what's the plan of action?' Hannah asked, polishing off the last morsel of her gateau.

Sally then related the telephone conversations after the two of them had spoken at her mother's house. An appointment had been made with DCI Winters the next morning at 11am at police headquarters at the Cobalt Business Park in North Tyneside to discuss the investigation more formally.

Following the meeting with Hannah, Sally decided to return home and start to make plans. The sooner she started on this investigation, the sooner she would find the answers to the questions swirling frantically around in her head.

On the short drive home she took in how things had changed in her village over the past decade and a bit. Buildings had sprung up where none had been before, but she was overjoyed to see her first school on Front Street still looking as it had all those years ago. She still recalled her first day at school; her mother leading her into the building by the hand and not knowing what it was or what was coming next or, indeed, what was about to happen to her in this strange place.

As she was rounding the corner into her mother's street she saw a very familiar car parked by the side of the road. 'What the–?' she began, and pulled onto the drive in front of the garage. She turned off the ignition and pulled the key out as quickly as she could, almost forgetting her bag in the footwell.

She could hear laughter coming from the living room as she opened the front door, then the sound of her mother's voice declaring 'Ah, here she is!'

'What on earth are you doing here?' she asked the man who had made himself comfortably at home beside her mother on the sofa.

'Well, is that any way to greet your partner?' Joe Burton asked her, laughing at her reaction to his rather impromptu arrival.

'But you're in Manchester!' she spluttered, regardless of the ridiculousness of that statement.

'Don't think so,' Burton retorted, looking himself up and down, 'unless life-size hologram projections are actually a real thing now!'

Mrs Fielding rose, laughing. 'I'm going to leave you two to sort this thing out by yourselves! If you need me for anything I'll be out in the conservatory.' She looked at her daughter then over to her detective partner, both of whom were just staring at one another like idiots. Sally had a look of complete incredulity on her face, but Joe Burton had a whimsical half-smile on his.

Young people! she smiled to herself as she walked away.

'Where are the cats?' Sally asked after what seemed like an eternity, looking around the room for her two feline pets, the ones he'd promised to look after for her during her sick leave.

'Hello, Joe, how are you doing today?' he said, replacing his own words with the greeting he was half-expecting from his partner. 'Don't worry, your cats are fine,' he reassured her, 'Jane and Sean are taking care of them while I'm up here.'

Apart from Joe Burton, she could think of nobody better than DC Jane Francis and her fiancé Sean Dylan to take care of

Sooty and Sweep in her absence, but it was Burton's presence here that she was concerned about at that moment.

'But what are you doing up here?'

'Well,' Burton rose until he was at eye level with her, 'after your telephone conversation with the boss yesterday she rang me. She thought that, under the circumstances, you might be keen of a little assistance ... so here I am.' He spread his arms out wide by his sides, but he could still see confusion on his co-worker's face. 'She said that she would be happy to fill in for me for the duration of your investigation. I think that she was eager to get her hands dirty one last time before the big retirement day if you ask me.' Still there was confusion on Sally's face; Burton spread his arms wider still. 'She said she could spare me, so here I am.'

'I know, I get that...'

At last, a response, Burton thought, letting his arms fall to their natural position. He knew that she had been through a lot in the past few weeks, so made a big allowance for that. As her usual self Sally Fielding was top of the game, and not the vague and confused person he now saw before him. Although, if some-body had come up to him and said that they had some informa-tion hitherto unknown about the death of a parent, he was sure that he too would be on a different planet by now.

'Oh, Joe, I'm so glad that you're here!' She flung her arms around him and gave him a huge bear hug. It took him by surprise, but he was happy to go along with it.

'So, what's the plan of action then?' he asked after she even-tually released the tight grip she had on him.

7

'Would you both like lunch?' Mrs Fielding popped her head around the door when she thought the moment was appropriate. As it was now after 1pm, and she had found herself becoming a little peckish whilst sitting in the conservatory she thought lunch for the three of them would be a good idea. She already knew Joe Burton to have a good heart; what he did for her daughter following her recent ordeal was nothing short of spectacular.

And she was happy to have Sally back in her life again. Thirteen years had been lost, but she had high hopes for their new-found relationship to be back on track for the future, even if her daughter returned to work in Manchester. After all, it was only a few hours' drive away at most. Her other daughter, Amanda, had been a regular visitor over the past week, and she was also happy to have her baby sister back in her life once again.

'I certainly would, if you're offering, that is!' Joe Burton was nothing if not predictable, and food was probably number one on the list of his most favourite things, so the offer of it in whatever form was met with great enthusiasm. Sally laughed out loud at his response.

'What?' He feigned shock as he knew that she knew what he was like around the subject. She picked up one of the cushions from the sofa and threw it at him, hitting him right in the face.

'Now, children!' her mother mock scolded them. 'I'm assuming that you can eat anything and are not like my finicky daughter over here?' She directed her question at Joe at the same time as she cocked a thumb over towards Sally.

'Absolutely. Stomach like cast iron,' he told her patting it, and she was more than happy to hear that.

'Right then, I'll give you both a shout when it's ready.'

The next half hour or so gave the two detectives time to catch up. Sally filled Joe in on what Hannah Sanderson had told her.

'And there's no reason to doubt this?' he had asked her, which she thought was an odd question.

'She's just recently retired from the force. Why should there be any doubt? Plus, she's Dad's former partner.'

'What I don't understand is,' he continued, 'why not mention all this at the time of your dad's death?'

'Well it's apparently in the official file, but the powers-that-be decided to withhold the full facts from the family.'

'You see, that's what I don't understand,' Joe continued. 'Yes, I can perhaps see why to a degree, but wouldn't your mother – and you and your sister come to that – want to know exactly what happened? I just can't see why they would want the cause of his heart attack to be kept from you all. I mean, having the heart attack in the manner in which he had it is so different from having it through natural causes. This amounts to manslaughter.'

Sally agreed with him: it had already crossed her mind the moment she heard it from Hannah. But the one thing that was important now was to find out how revered author Jonas Burke managed to describe the scene in great detail – and even more importantly, who it was that related that precise information on to him.

There was so much detail that it had to have come from somebody who was there that fateful day, who saw the whole thing. Or the information had to have come from the official police file. Either way, this was a serious matter regardless of how long ago it was. Sally was determined that she would get to the bottom of it.

This wasn't just a case of her carrying out her duties, or of her avenging her father's death; in Sally's mind finding out this person's identity was the culmination of all her training as a police officer and why she had joined the police force in the first place. Karma. Yes, that was it … fate, like it was just meant to be.

Over lunch, which consisted of a chicken salad for Joe and her mother and a cheese salad for herself, Sally avoided all talk of the investigation for her mother's sake. It was also during lunch that Mrs Fielding asked where Joe was staying whilst up in the north east.

'Well I'm not really sure yet, Mrs Fielding–'

'Oh please, call me Christine,' she interrupted him.

'All right then, Christine, I just grabbed a few things and hit the road, but I believe that there's a good hotel up on the business park next to the cinema.'

'Oh no, you don't want to go booking yourself into a hotel, Joe. I've got a spare bedroom and you're very welcome to stay with us for the duration of your time here.'

Joe exchanged looks with Sally. Was he looking for her permission? She really wasn't sure what the glance meant but she gave her thoughts on her mother's suggestion. 'That's actually a good idea, Mum, if you don't mind that is?' For one thing, it would save him money for she had no idea how long their investigation would take, and another, she'd be pleased to have him in the house.

The family home had been without any male occupancy since her father passed away, something her mother had told her during her convalescence, and she could think of no other man than her partner to take up temporary residence. Sally had been a bit concerned for her mother when she'd told her that there hadn't been anybody else since her father had died, but then she'd said something which made her fully understand.

'Some people are just irreplaceable,' she'd told her when she noticed the sadness of the situation in her daughter's eyes, which moved Sally more than she could say. Yes, her father had been irreplaceable, not only to her mother but also to herself and her sister.

Mrs Fielding said to Joe, 'I'll make the bed up this afternoon for you.'

By mid-afternoon, after lunch had gone down, Sally suggested a walk around the village for all three of them. Her mother declined, and also refused help with the dishes when they offered. 'Go out and get some fresh air in your lungs,' she said. She knew that they'd want to talk shop about whatever it was they were working on.

'Yes, I'm game,' Joe enthused, already up out of his seat and reaching for his coat. 'I'd like to take a look around the place you grew up in!'

'It's not that big a place, you know,' Sally told him, not quite knowing what he was expecting to see. 'This isn't like your hometown; it's just a semi-rural village surrounded by fields and horses, and a cricket club.'

'Ah, but you do have a cinema complex.'

'That we do,' Sally admitted, 'but it's not like Leicester Square or anything.'

He laughed, and she wondered exactly what it was she'd said that had amused him so much. Her expression must have spoken volumes as he replied, 'You're saying "we": it's as if you never left the place all those years ago.'

'One week back and I'm already a native again, it seems!' She reached for her coat from one of the hooks beside the front door and put it on. As she'd already been outside this morning she knew that it wasn't very warm out there, so she also took a beanie hat, scarf and a pair of gloves with her. 'All right then,' she said to him, looking him up and down and wondering why he never felt the cold like she did, 'off we go on the magical mystery tour of Boldon.'

8

Nothing much had changed; the row of shops beside the metro station were pretty much as they had always been, with a few new businesses here and there; and her old dentist had moved into the former bank premises at the top of Station Road near Black's Corner and the main road junction traffic lights. Also, there was a restaurant on the corner where she remembered a print supply business back in her day. Her grandmother told her that the little corner shop was once a small grocery store run by a lady called Mrs Black – hence the name of the corner.

'This is nice,' Joe said as they were walking along. She had to admit that it was. Never in her wildest dreams could she have imagined herself once again walking around the place where she had spent her formative years, her Wonderland-loving years where she was Alice Liddell, slayer of the Jabberwock, chasing the white rabbit around the rose garden in Grange Park while it stopped to look at its pocket watch before running away from her again.

And there she was, harking back to the events of the past few weeks. It was going to take some getting over, that was for sure, but she knew that she must strive to overcome the memory of the whole ordeal. They managed to get as far as the cinema on their stroll and had, perhaps not unexpectedly, stopped in at Starbucks where Joe had been impressed by the coffee, and they simply sat and chatted about William Fielding – the man, the police officer and the father.

By the time they returned home, after a short detour to buy Sally a pair of black work trousers and a couple of tops at the neighbouring superstore, it was fast approaching dinner time, and the light had gone an hour or so previously. Mrs Fielding already had the living room lights and the flickering log-effect gas fire turned on when they got back to the house.

'I was wondering if you both might like a takeaway tonight?' she said as soon as they entered. Sally knew one person in particular who would be keen on that and waited for her mother to utter the classic question when they both said yes. 'Now what will it be, Indian or Chinese?'

As it had only been a matter of weeks since she had been there, Sally remembered the way to Police Headquarters in North Tyneside with great accuracy, and offered to drive Joe's car the following day. He was glad of the break and the offer, and let her drive without any objection. Long-distance driving wasn't his thing. He had loathed the journey up from Manchester twenty-four hours earlier, but he had overcome his dislike to help his partner. That was the main thing. He admired her, and Jack Summers for that matter, for enduring that long drive through Europe recently; even though he had encouraged them both and tried to make it sound like a relatively easy task, he knew that if he'd been in their shoes he'd have been tearing his hair out with the stress of it all. So full marks, and extreme respect, to both of them for managing to get through it in one piece.

Fixing her mobile phone into the holder on Joe's dashboard, she put Hannah Sanderson's postcode into the maps app, hit the directions button then the blue start arrow. A pleasant female voice came from the device advising her which direction to set off in. Although she did know her own village quite well, well enough to get Joe Burton to a coffee shop the previous day, beyond that was an entirely different matter – especially when it came to sitting behind the wheel of a car.

She had barely started driving before leaving home to go to Manchester, so side roads and short cuts in this part of the country were completely unknown to her. Manchester, yes, she could manoeuvre her car around there without any problem at all. Having spent more than a decade driving around the place she had come to know virtually every back street and out-of-the-way location, and she had built up quite a collection of short cuts to get her from one location to another. But here, no. She had spent nearly all ... correction ... *all* of the past week sitting in her mother's conservatory, surfacing only for meals and sleep. She hadn't even sat in a car until she went out to meet Hannah for coffee the day before.

The seventeen-minute journey took them through Boldon Colliery, Jarrow and then on to Hebburn, stopping right outside the number she'd been given in Bicester Grove. Sally had called ahead to say that they were coming, and Hannah already had her coat on and was looking out of her living room window when the car pulled up outside the row of four terraced houses.

'Nice,' Joe said, looking around him, 'they seem quite new.'

'Looks that way,' Sally agreed.

After a brief introduction, Hannah sat in the back behind Joe and they continued towards the Tyne Tunnel, the underwater roadway that links North and South Tyneside.

'What, this is underwater?' Joe asked incredulously as they began their journey through the one-mile tunnel.

'Partly, and you can see the water coming in through the walls a bit further up,' Hannah joked, but Joe was horrified.

'Whaaaaat?' He almost shrieked, turning around in his seat to look at the woman behind him.

'I'm only kidding!' She laughed on seeing the expression on his face. 'The tunnel has been operational since 1968, and it hasn't sprung a leak yet.'

Joe turned to face the front windscreen again, hoping that nobody had seen the beads of sweat he could feel beginning to form on his forehead. He wasn't overly fond of water, so he stared straight ahead of him, quite literally desperate to see the light at the end of the tunnel.

DCI Paul Winters met all three in his office on the second floor of the police headquarters in the Cobalt Business Park.

'Nice to see you again,' he said to DS Fielding, 'and a pleasure to meet you, detective inspector,' the latter directed towards her partner. The man had a firm handshake, one which Burton appreciated. To him, a firm hand was indicative of a strong, decisive person, and in this line of work having a strong leader was vital to staff morale.

'Hannah!' His greeting towards former DI Sanderson was more familiar. Sally knew that they had worked together in the past; she had spoken very highly of him and it appeared that the appreciation was a mutual one. They hugged briefly, then Winters invited them to all sit around his desk on the three chairs already set out for them.

He sat opposite and cleared his throat. 'As you can well appreciate, the contents of Mr Jonas Burke's novel is causing a great deal of concern. Not only does it reveal a security leak of our own in-house records, but also throws a different light on your father's death, DS Fielding.' He looked towards Sally. She had been staring down at both hands clasped firmly on her lap but looked up at the sound of her name and nodded.

Winters continued, eyes still on her. 'You have, of course, access to all the files and cases that were being worked on at the time by your father and DI Sanderson here. This matter is very serious and one which we cannot afford to take lightly.'

They were words DS Fielding had never expected to hear as both she and her family had accepted what they had been told about William Fielding's sudden death. She was grateful, but still felt reluctant to tell her mother about anything that was going on. She must have suspected something was up – of course she must, she wasn't stupid – but as a former police officer's wife she never asked until told, regardless of the situation.

'I've also arranged for an office to be set up for you just along the corridor so that you can work here on site.'

'That's very kind of you, Paul,' Hannah said, doing away with the formality of referring to her ex-colleague by his official title. As she was no longer a serving member of the force, she was perfectly entitled to address him by his given name.

'Was the serial killer you were chasing that night ever caught, Hannah?' Burton asked her, to which she shook her head.

'No, unfortunately not. I don't know if it was because he came so close to capture, but that was the last we heard of him and the case went cold after that.'

Winters then resumed. 'As we're looking back to the year 2005 everything should now be computerised and on the database, so all the information you need will already be loaded on there. However, if you do need access to the paper files, including your dad's service record, DS Fielding, there is a library in the basement which will help you with this.

'Thank you,' DI Burton said.

Winters sat back in his chair. 'What do we know about this Jonas Burke? Hannah, you've read his book. Is there any information in the book itself about him?'

'Well I haven't read it all; as I said to Sally, I only got to chapter eighteen and was so shocked by what I read that I didn't get any further. I think that there's a very brief biography, but nothing other than that.'

'We could always contact the publisher,' Fielding suggested, which seemed the most sensible thing to do as a starting point. 'I'm sure that they'll be able to put us in contact with the man or, at the very least, with his agent.'

'Good idea, sergeant,' Winters said, tapping his pen on the desk. 'That's the way forward, I think: see what the man has to say for himself and then take it from there. Whoever has been feeding him this information is in serious breach of the Data Protection Act and we have to act accordingly.'

As the meeting appeared to reach a natural conclusion, Winters picked up the phone and pressed a button on the receiver, connecting him to his secretary.

'Gemma, could you please show our colleagues to the room that's been set up along the corridor. Thanks.'

The young girl, who couldn't be any more than twenty, appeared almost immediately in the doorway. *Quite young for such an elevated position*, Fielding thought. Paul Winters rose to his feet and shook each of their hands in turn. 'Don't forget, if you need me, please don't hesitate to knock on my door at any time.'

'We'll do that,' Burton told him, and led the group out of the room, all three following the secretary to what was to be their base for the duration of the investigation.

9

The room assigned to them was big enough to hold three desks, which were arranged facing one another in a triangle. That way everyone could easily see the other and not have to turn around to hold a conversation. Each of the desks had a telephone, monitor and keyboard. And there was a printer in the corner should they need to print off any information. On one of the walls adjacent to the full-length window a long console table had been set up with a kettle, a jar of coffee, sugar sachets and a two litre carton of milk. But what joyfully caught the eye of both Fielding and Burton was a Tassimo coffee machine, complete with an assortment of coffee pods stacked up beside it in a metal dispenser. The two detectives looked at one another and smiled, especially as Hannah muttered, 'Lovely, we can drink as much tea as we want.' Their thoughts at that moment weren't on tea, but on plugging that machine in and firing it up.

Before starting on any of the record files, they did an internet search for the author Jonas Burke. There was plenty of information about him and, more pertinent to them, his agent's contact details.

'Here we go then,' Burton said, picking up the phone and dialling the London number. It was answered within three rings by a softly-spoken young man. When Burton announced who he was, he was connected to a Mr Douglas Langley, the man directly responsible for Burke's affairs.

'But what does this have to do with my client?' Langley asked after hearing Burton's request.

'It's imperative that we speak to him about some information which has come to light during an enquiry.'

The line went silent for a moment, which prompted Burton to ask if the man was still there.

'Yes, yes, I'm here,' Langley announced, 'but let me have a word with him first and get him to ring you, if that's all right?'

'Certainly,' Burton told him and gave him the police HQ telephone number along with the extension he was calling from. Suspecting that Langley would be checking out that he was who he claimed he was, he also gave him telephone numbers for DCI Winters and DCI Ambleton as people to contact to confirm his identity. 'I'm currently working with Northumbria Police in North Tyneside on secondment from Manchester; my boss will confirm that for you.'

'No, it wasn't that. I didn't doubt you,' Langley began, but Burton knew otherwise. He would have done the same thing in his position. Burke was an international bestselling author, and any overly enthusiastic fan could have found his agent's telephone number as easily as he had just done and called claiming to be a police officer in order to speak to the man.

'I'll expect a call soon then.' It was more of a statement than a question from Burton, and Langley told him that it would be within the hour.

True to his word, Langley managed to locate his client on his book tour. When the call came through, Burton put it on loudspeaker so his team could listen in.

'Jonas Burke speaking,' the author began. Hannah Sanderson recognised the voice immediately, so could confirm that it was indeed him who was calling. She nodded her head in affirmation. 'That's him,' she whispered to the others.

'Mr Burke, my name is Detective Inspector Joe Burton and I'm currently working with Northumbria Police. I was wanting to speak to you about where you get your background information for your books.'

'Yes, my agent informed me of that. What is it exactly that you want to know about it?'

'Well, for starters, do you have someone who does your research for you?'

'I have a researcher, yes,' Burke confirmed.

'And does he have access to police records?'

'Not that I know of. Look, what exactly is this about, detective? I'm a little bit confused by it all.'

No more than we are, Burton thought, but did not convey that observation to Burke. 'It's come to light,' he told him, 'that the details of a crime scene in your latest book are identical to something that happened here in the north east thirteen years ago.'

'I hire my researcher to go through public records, newspapers and such, and pick out incidences of crime. He prints them off and I put them into a file then introduce them into my books as and when I need specific details. All the crimes I describe are based on these findings; I change all the relevant parts, of course, so that my descriptions are not identical to the actual crimes, but that's how I get all the background information.'

'You see, that's just it,' Burton continued. 'The information on one specific crime in your current book looks like it's come straight from a police report, almost word perfect in fact–'

Burke interrupted, 'But I've just told you how–'

Burton likewise interrupted him. 'The specifics weren't released in the press. Neither are they in any public records; they were in-house only, Mr Burke, not for public knowledge. For this reason I need to speak to your researcher as a matter of some urgency.'

'I see,' Burke said after a moment's silence. 'Of course. I'll give you his number.'

Fielding ran across to the copier and opened the paper feed drawer, took a sheet from the tray and put it down in front of her colleague. Burton quickly jotted down the name and number Burke gave him then thanked the author for his co-operation. He also wrote down the mobile number showing on the display, which he assumed to be the author's personal phone. It would certainly come in handy as, doubtless, they would need to contact him again.

'Although,' Burke said as an afterthought, 'if you're talking thirteen years ago then you'll have little luck on that front I'm afraid.'

Burton's high hopes suddenly sank to the ground like a lead balloon. 'And why is that?' he asked the author, deflated.

'My previous researcher died about five years ago. However, his son took over; his is the number I've just given you, and he may very well be able to help you ... or not, as the case may be. Will that be all, detective?'

Hannah Sanderson suddenly went off the man. At first he'd seemed to be co-operative, but his last snide comment threw a completely different light on him for her. 'Arrogant bastard!' she exclaimed after Burton had hung up.

'I agree,' said Fielding, who was a little less than impressed with the author herself.

You watch him searching for information to use, his dexterous fingers

working quickly and effectively on the keyboard until he finds something of value.

It could be of use next week or a few years hence, but it will certainly feature at some time or another. He is far more skilful than you could ever be, especially when he can go in and change the way things were into the way he wants them to be. Now that's talent!

Manipulative and very possibly illegal, but talent all the same.

He tells you not to mind what he's doing as he's doing it for good reasons; reasons beneficial to both of you.

So you obey. You are helpless not to.

Alan Bedlington was more approachable than his employer, although he wasn't sure how he could possibly be of assistance to the police. 'I just collect information from press releases and library records, depending upon which part of the country Mr Burke wants to set his books in,' he explained over the telephone. 'My father showed me the ropes when he became ill, and recommended me to Mr Burke.'

'So you're doing the job just as your father did before you then?'

'Exactly.'

'So do you, or did your father, ever have access to official police records?'

'What do you mean?' Bedlington asked, becoming more defensive.

Burton felt that to be a fairly straightforward question, but repeated it in a different way. 'Official police files: do you have access to or know anyone who can provide you with information from them?'

'No, of course not!' The researcher's tone changed dramatically. 'Like I said, I just gather information from records in the public domain. I couldn't get access even if I wanted to, as I don't know anybody in the police force. In any way, I would have thought that to be illegal, using confidential material like that. My father certainly wouldn't have done that and neither would I for that matter.'

Burton looked over at his partner and then to Hannah, feeling that what had initially seemed to be a hopeful line of enquiry was proving less than productive. From their expressions he could see that they agreed with him. Bedlington had seemed genuinely shocked and upset by his integrity being questioned, and Burton needed to reassure him that was not what he had intended.

'No, I didn't think for one moment that either of you would have, and I'm certainly not suggesting it. I'm just covering all angles, that's all. I'm sure you understand?'

'Yes, of course,' Bedlington replied less defensively.

'A couple more questions if I may? Does anyone work with you on this; somebody who comes in and gives you assistance?'

'No, it's just me.'

To be honest, Burton hadn't expected immediate results on the very first morning on the job, but at the same time he hadn't expected such a dead end as the one he was facing now. Burton's heart sank. But then he had a thought. Having a look at the files might be very beneficial, as there could be something in the researcher's records that was relevant to their enquiry. 'One last question then. Would you allow us access to your files, Mr Bedlington?'

'Yes, of course. Do you want me to send them all to you? I do have quite a lot, as you can imagine.'

'Where is it that you live?' Burton really couldn't imagine the size of his collection as he had no idea how much background information an author would need to have in reserve. He did think that it would be beneficial to view all the files Bedlington had now rather than having to wait a day at least for them to be delivered to the office.

'Cambridgeshire,' Bedlington replied. 'In a village called Hardwick.'

'In that case it may be better if we come down to view them ourselves; would that be acceptable to you?'

'Yes, of course. When would you want to come?'

'The sooner the better, I think,' Burton told him. 'How about tomorrow? If we leave in the morning we could be there early afternoon.'

As all parties were in agreement, Joe Burton wrote down Bedlington's home address and thanked him for his assistance.

'I'm not entirely sure what we will find,' he told the others, 'but I think it warrants seeing the files first-hand.' Fielding and Hannah couldn't agree with him more. 'But, Hannah,' he continued, regretting that he would have to say it, 'I think only Sally and I should do this part; if you want to continue here by all means do so and we'll catch up once we've both returned.'

'What would you like me to do while you're both away then?' Although hiding it well, Hannah was furious. She had alerted them to something being wrong in the first place, and here they were excluding her from a vital part of the investigation.

Burton thought for a moment as he hadn't really considered them having to separate, but eventually came up with an idea. 'I tell you what you could do, Hannah, if you don't mind?'

'Go ahead,' she said a little coldly.

'It might be a good idea to get some sort of a list of all the crimes in Jonas Burke's books and compare them to the records Alan Bedlington holds.'

'I don't think I could go through all of his books in a day!' Hannah exclaimed, more than a little overwhelmed by the prospect of having to do it. First the exclusion and now this.

'No, no, no, I didn't mean for you to do it manually,' Burton reassured her. 'If he's that popular it must all be written down somewhere? A fan site, perhaps? There must be something out there on the internet that can help us.'

'Right, I'll do that then, and as for coming in, I can quite easily do research from home while you're both away.' Hannah was nothing if not polite, and managed to successfully hide the frustration she was feeling.

'We really appreciate that, Hannah,' Sally told her, grateful that she was dedicating herself to this as much as they were. What she couldn't see was Hannah's anger bubbling away under the surface, and how that anger might have a detrimental effect on the case in days to come.

10

'I've just been enjoying being home, being mothered,' said Sally. 'I never realised I missed Boldon, and home... and my family.'

Burton had enjoyed the drive until that point. They'd had a good run down, and it looked like it would be nearer three hours than the four promised by the route planner they'd used, even including a pit stop for coffee. But now it crossed his mind that Fielding might want to return to the north east, to seek employment with the police force up here just to be with her family. It was unfounded, he knew, as she'd not even mentioned that it was on her mind; but he'd got it into his head that he might lose his partner to the land of her birth, and that frightened him. Mainly because he didn't want to lose her. He started to think about the connotations of that. Did he not want to lose her because he thought that she was the best police officer he had ever had the pleasure to work with, or did he not want to lose her because of the person she was and because he had become so attached to her? They hadn't even dated, and here he was worrying as if they were already a couple and happily married. Was that what he ultimately wanted from her, to be married and settled down with a couple of miniature versions of themselves running around the house?

His ruminations were beginning to scare him, so to distract his thoughts he asked Sally if he should put on an audiobook, and she was more than happy for him to do so.

'As long as it isn't one of Jonas Burke's,' she added quickly.

By the time they approached Lincolnshire the landscape began to change, and the undulating hills of Yorkshire gradually gave way to the Fens. The marshy region of eastern England, mostly around The Wash and parts of Lincolnshire, Cambridgeshire, Norfolk and Suffolk, is low-lying, and in some parts no more than ten metres above sea level, so the panoramic vista is that of flattened land as far as the eye can see.

Eventually, they reached their destination of Hardwick and parked up on Cambridge Road right outside Alan Bedlington's picturesque Dutch bungalow. Fielding liked the architectural feature, and had seen many like it in her mother's neighbouring village of Cleadon. The style gave regular bungalows an extra floor by utilising the loft space and fitting louvred windows into the sloping roof.

Burton turned off the ignition and the first thing that hit them was the silence. The second thing was the wonderful fresh smell of the great outdoors when they opened the car doors. The clean, unpolluted air only added to the charm of the place.

The front of Bedlington's home faced a row of high trees, with the occasional gap here and there showing farmland beyond. Fields, which in high summer must be filled with colour and crops, now lay bare and furrowed. It was quite the idyllic spot, hidden away from an unsuspecting world.

'I'd love to live in a place like this,' Burton told his companion. 'Imagine coming home to this peacefulness after some of the sights and sounds we see and hear each day.'

Fielding was likewise impressed. It was not unlike the semi-rural surroundings of the place she had grown up in. Though Cambridgeshire was much flatter than South Tyneside, she could imagine herself living here.

But back to business. She opened up the back door of the car and reached inside for her laptop. Being an accomplished typist who could do sixty-plus words a minute, it was her preferred method of note-taking and so much better than trying to decipher hurried scribbles in a jotter. She couldn't cope with having to depend on the type of notebook Burton always carried around with him.

They had expected Alan Bedlington to be an older man, so when they were greeted at the door by a fresh-faced youth in his early twenties they were both taken by surprise. They thought him to be Alan Bedlington's son, but he dispelled that idea by greeting them with, 'Detectives, you've made good time. Please come on in. I've got everything ready for you.'

The house had a traditional front and so the ultra-modern interior came as a bit of a surprise. It was more lad's pad, like one of the trendy lofts in Manchester, than country cottage. Alan Bedlington's interests outside of his work appeared to be modern technology. The high-tech equipment made up for the sparsely furnished living room. The main point of focus was a TV screen on the wall above the fireplace. It must have been at least eighty inches in diameter. Burton was impressed and let out a long whistle. Bedlington seemed delighted by his reaction.

'That is about as big as one of my living room walls,' the detective told him, gazing wistfully at its magnificence.

'Great, isn't it?' A huge grin spread across his cherub-like face. He was obviously happy to have found someone with a like-minded appreciation.

Fielding watched the two men together; both standing drooling over a black rectangle on the wall ... and it wasn't even turned on. *Goodness knows what they would be like if it had been,* she thought. *Now I like to watch TV, but come on guys!* She coughed gently, bringing Burton back to the real world and the reason for their being there in the first place.

'Right. Yes.' He cast a hasty sideways look at his partner then back to the researcher. 'Okay, Mr Bedlington, I think we'd better get down to business.'

'Of course ... but she's a prize, isn't she?'

Fielding despaired. He was even referring to the thing as female.

Bedlington led them through into another room, which was set up as an office. He walked over to his desk and opened one of the large bottom drawers, bringing out two bulging A4 box folders. Each were so full that they could see edges of paper trying to make their escape. He indicated that the detectives take one each.

'And they're just ideas for murders in his books?' Fielding asked incredulously, taking the one from the top. She almost dropped it; it was that heavy.

'Yes they are!' Bedlington beamed, evidently proud of his work and that of his father before him.

'So when did your father start working for Mr Burke?' Burton asked, taking his file and sitting down on one of the armchairs.

'When Mr Burke started writing his novels,' Bedlington told them. 'He and Dad used to work together on a national newspaper in London, and they were good friends outside work. Dad was an archivist for the company and Mr Burke was a sports columnist at the time. I seem to recall as well that Burke had studied computer science at university prior to that, so not sure how the progression to journalism came in. Unhappy with his choice perhaps? I really don't know. When he decided to start writing his books he asked Dad if he would help him with the research and stuff. Apparently, my mother thought it was a bit of a gamble at the time, especially with a young family to feed – I was only six at that point and my younger sister was three. She couldn't see how writing books could make any sort of living for anyone, but she was proved wrong about that in a relatively short space of time. Mr Burke's first book was an international best seller, and his subsequent books have all been successes, so Dad's gamble well and truly paid off – and for me too, as I've taken over where he left off.'

'Sounds like a dream come true, for all concerned,' Burton said, opening the file and gazing hopelessly at its contents. They'd never get through one of these in a day let alone two. Then he had an idea that just might save them some time. 'Might we be able to take photographs of all of these?' He asked their owner.

'I don't see why not,' Bedlington said to him, 'as long as you destroy them when you've finished with them. As you can appreciate, it's taken almost twenty years to gather all of these together and would give someone an unfair advantage if they fell into the wrong hands. If you can give me that assurance, then yes, you may.'

'I'll make sure that they're properly taken care of.' Burton appreciated his reasons for being cautious, although he knew that he would have to hold on to them until the end of their investigation.

'Do you know if Mr Burke had or has a police advisor?' Fielding asked, beginning to take the contents from the file but keeping them in the same order.

'I believe so, but neither I nor my father before me was ever privy to that.'

'Why is that then?' She wondered why that was deemed so secretive.

'I did ask him the reason for that once, when I first started doing the work, but he said that due to the delicate nature of it, it was probably better that he kept that one to himself. To be honest, I couldn't see why as I was working for him and knew that his work was confidential, but I respected his decision and simply left it at that. But about what you asked me yesterday, I can't see how he managed to gain access to police records unless, that is, his police advisor provided him with that.'

'You see, that's it,' Fielding told him, 'if that was the case then that advisor has breached confidentiality.'

'I see that,' Bedlington told her, realising the full implications of it. 'All I can suggest, in that case, is asking Mr Burke himself as I can't give you the answer to it.'

'Oh we intend to,' Burton chipped in, still looking at the pile in front of him. 'Okay then, Fielding, let's start copying these documents.'

'I'll leave you alone then,' the young lad said and turned to leave the room. But before doing so he turned and asked them if he could get them a drink.

'Coffee would be nice,' Burton told him. They'd already had one earlier during their mid-way break with a quick snack, but that was an hour or so ago and by now were both in dire need of another.

'I only have ground, would that be okay? Or I have a coffee machine and could knock up something more fancy for you if you'd prefer that?'

More than, Burton thought, knowing that his partner would be thinking the same.

11

Even though the sheets of A4 paper in the files belonging to Jonas Burke's researcher were single-sided ones, the whole process of photographing each in turn took over two hours, by which time two more coffees apiece had been very kindly brought to them by their host, and drunk.

'I think that's it,' Joe Burton declared upon reaching the final sheet, and turning the whole pile over he placed it back in the box in the same order as it had come out.

'Me too,' Fielding echoed, finishing up at about the same time as her colleague.

Alan Bedlington had been sitting in the living room playing a video game, if the sound of gunfire emanating from the huge TV's speakers was anything to go by, but hearing their voices paused it and came through.

'All done?' he asked seeing the box files now closed and on the top of the desk.

'Yes, we are, thank you.' There was one last question, however, that Burton wanted to ask him before they left to head back up north. 'Tell me,' he began. 'Has Mr Burke used all of the crimes listed in the files in his novels?'

'All of them?' Bedlington pondered. 'Why, no, I doubt that. His latest novel is his twenty-sixth and usually they have up to five crimes in them, so there's a lot more information in there for him to use for future novels.'

'And you said that you get the information from newspapers and such?' Burton continued.

'Newspapers, magazines, even crime shows on TV at times, and Mr Burke adds his own ideas too. His are the ones that you'll find handwritten in there as he just usually scribbles down any ideas that come to him and sends them off to me.'

'And what about the incident in his latest novel, the part where the villain tasers the police officer, where did that come from?' Sally Fielding had been quietly listening to the conversation, but this was one question that she had to ask.

'That was one of his own ideas, as I recall.'

You can see that he's agitated about something but you're uncertain what it is. You want to ask him, but you know that you won't get an answer as he doesn't take questions well.

So you have to simply observe until he finds what he has been looking for. He's always good at looking for things. Once found, he picks up the telephone and dials the number on the piece of paper. Assistance is on its way.

As soon as they started their long journey back Sally got out her phone and began looking at the photographs.

'Hey, hey!' Burton began when he saw out of the corner of his eye what she was doing. 'We can leave all that until the morning you know; it's not necessary to go through them right now.' However, he knew exactly why she was doing it. The answer to how Burke had obtained the information may very well be in there somewhere, and she didn't want to waste one minute in trying to find it.

'I know but–' she began, but Burton stopped her before she could say any more.

'We can upload them to the computer tomorrow and spend all day going over them, plus we'll have Hannah to help us as well. I know that to say you're keen is an understatement, but we can get a better look at them on a screen that's much larger than your phone or mine.'

'You're right,' she agreed, slipping her phone into her bag.

He smiled. He didn't want her worn out, especially after her recent ordeal, plus she was still supposed to be on sick leave, though Ambleton had said that she would sort that out before they began the investigation. 'I don't know about you, but I'm feeling peckish,' he said, casting her a cheeky grin.

Fielding laughed, and Burton was overjoyed to hear the old familiar laugh that he knew so well. 'When are you not?' she quipped, but had to admit that she was as well.

'We'll keep an eye out for somewhere that looks good and pop in then.'

They didn't have to wait too long, for as soon as they'd come off the A14 and re-joined the A1 they saw a billboard sign advertising a very pleasant-looking pit stop just south of Stamford. Taking the slip road where indicated, it led them to a charming country pub with a welcoming exterior. The interior didn't fail to impress either. It was decorated in an olde worlde style complete with dark wood beams and a real log fire roaring away in a grate in the dining area.

The break did them both good and set them up for the

remainder of the journey home to Sally's mother's house in Boldon. Knowing her mother, Sally fully expected that there'd be another meal waiting for them when they got back, or perhaps another takeaway like the previous evening. She felt full, but another few hours on the road would put paid to that. *Must be the northern air*, she thought, as she'd had quite an appetite for the duration of her stay up there. Once back in Manchester she'd be back to her usual appetite and food intake. At that moment she thought about her two cats and hoped that they would be all right with Jane and Sean, but deep down knew that they would be. Apart from Joe looking after them, those two were a good second choice to take care of her precious pets.

Both woke bright and early the next morning, eager to face the day ahead of them with a renewed passion. After battling through early morning Tyne Tunnel traffic and arriving at their office, they had all the photographs taken from Alan Bedlington's files to load up onto the computer with the prospect of spending the rest of the day scrutinising them to glean the tiniest piece of information which might be of assistance. Anything would help; a hint at his police advisor's contact name if not full-on disclosure would be most beneficial, or at the very least other information about the events surrounding William Fielding's death.

Hannah had texted the previous evening to say that she wouldn't require a lift as she intended to drive herself in early. This whole thing was personal to her too, and she would be as keen as Fielding was – and also Burton – to find the person or persons responsible for her partner's death. And they weren't wrong.

Hannah was already on the computer when they entered the

room and sprung to her feet as soon as she saw them. 'I've got quite a bit of news to tell you!' she declared, flushed with excitement.

'So do we,' Fielding told her, and related the events of the previous day.

Hannah politely sat and listened, but she was furious that Sally had jumped in and cut her short. She'd gone out of her way to come in early to help out and that was how they'd thanked her. When Sally finished telling her their news she then told them her own.

'I did quite a bit of research on Jonas Burke yesterday. As you said, there was no way we could sit and read through all of his twenty-six novels, so as you suggested I tried to find information on the internet.'

'Go on,' Burton said, becoming very interested. He was eager to learn what she'd turned up.

'Mr Burke is a very popular author, mega popular in fact, and has a wide fan base all over the world, and that was how I thought of it. Surely one or several of his keener fans would be able to provide us with all the information we need without us having to trawl through all the novels ourselves. So I looked online for any groups or names that stood out. And that was when I found her. Doris Mendelson is Burke's number one super-fan, and that's putting it very mildly indeed, and, fortunately for us, she lives not too far away from here up in Northumberland.'

'How is she such a super-fan then?' Fielding asked. She'd always been a bit wary of these followers of so-called famous people as what they did seemed to border on stalking. The fascination with the rich and famous was totally lost on her, and akin to people taking an unhealthy interest in murderers.

Hannah enlightened them. 'She's read all of his books, has made a list of all the crimes featured in them – although for the life of me I can't figure out why, but have to say I'm glad of it right now – and has a mountain of information about crime scenes and locations and all the characters he has in each book.'

Burton shared Fielding's opinion about over-enthusiastic fans. 'These people...' he muttered, shaking his head.

'I know where you're coming from,' Fielding told him, 'but this could be just what we're looking for. If she has all this information readily to hand, then it has to hold something for us to work with.'

'I agree,' Hannah enthused, 'there has to be something in there that will be of use to us.'

'Okay then,' Burton agreed. 'Have you been in contact with her?'

'No, not personally, but I asked a DC to make the appointment, and Mrs Mendelson says she can see us tomorrow morning.'

12

'Thank you,' said Burton, moving to take the file on William Fielding's death from Hannah.

But the retired detective kept hold of the papers. 'I'm okay to read through them and summarise for you.'

'I'd like to look myself,' said Burton firmly. He did not feel comfortable with Hannah or Fielding having to read through the notes about the incident which killed William Fielding and had asked whoever found them to hand them over to him.

'He was my–' Hannah stopped herself and gave the folder to Burton.

As he read through the notes there wasn't anything more than they already knew; nothing to imply or indicate who had supplied the information to Burke in the first place – which was very frustrating. The only thing that caught his eye was a capital letter W here and there in the text and presumably written by Burke's own hand, which could quite feasibly be a clue to his contact but, then again, it might not. It could easily stand for 'witness' or anything else for that matter. Clearly the author had kept the identity of his police advisor very close to his chest, hidden even in his detailed notes. He hoped that their visit to Doris Mendelson the next day might be more profitable.

Doris Mendelson lived just north of Hexham in the charming village of Acomb. Sitting idyllically in the Northumbrian countryside and surrounded by the looming Cheviot Hills, it was still picturesque at this time of the year. The surrounding fields lay bare, hopefully expectant of regrowth to come in the spring and summer months ahead.

As Burton parked up beside the lady's home, Fielding and Sanderson saw curtains and blinds twitch in the surrounding houses in the cul-de-sac. It appeared that strangers were rarities in this part of the country and so were of great interest and curiosity.

Doris Mendelson herself was not how they'd expected a fangirl to look. They were met by a woman in perhaps her mid to late thirties with a young toddler in tow.

'Ms Mendelson?' Burton asked with a degree of incredulity.

The woman laughed at his apparent shock. 'Not what you expected then!'

'No, not really,' he admitted.

As she ushered them indoors her young daughter kept very close to her side, almost hiding from view behind her mother's back. Her large blue eyes watched every movement they made. Like the rest of the village, it seemed that she too was very curious about these strange people who had come into her home. She was a pretty little thing, with long dark curly hair cascading down her back. Remnants of the bar of chocolate she had been eating prior to their arrival were still evident on her face and hands.

'It's Mrs, actually,' she told him, 'but please, call me Doris. And this is Jemima.'

She led them into the living room, which was a mixture of modern and traditional furnishings, and indicated with a gesture that they should all take a seat on the large curved sofa. Before being seated herself, she picked up a wet wipe from a nearby open packet and rubbed it across her daughter's mouth and hands. Now clean, the little girl smiled at the visitors, the wide grin almost extending from ear to ear. The strangers felt like they had been accepted.

'I gather that you wish to see my collection.' It wasn't a question, neither was it a statement; it was simply a proclamation of pride on Doris Mendelson's part.

Burton had never met anyone like her before. He'd heard about obsessive fans, but the ones he'd come across had taken their passion to an unprecedented level and often acted in an outrageous way that occasionally led to arrest. But here was a self-admitted passionate fan who did not fall into that category. She appeared to be, well, normal. 'Absolutely,' Burton said, wondering just where she kept all of this as nothing was evident in this room.

'We really don't get many visitors to this part of the world, but I do get the odd fan drop in now and again; mostly people I've come into contact with on the internet and who wish to get a first-hand look at it. I even get a reporter or two coming in from time to time to write an article on me. Like you, they seem surprised both by me and the lack of anything on display.' She laughed, rising from the chair. She picked up her little girl and deposited her in the playpen behind the sofa. 'Stay here while Mummy goes upstairs to show these nice people her special room.' But Jemima had already begun playing and was now oblivious to anything else going on around her.

'Come with me,' Doris said, and led all three out into the

hallway. The flight of stairs took them up to the first floor, and the flight beyond that led up to the attic space. Opening the door, Doris led them into her pride and joy then stood back while they looked around. 'Please, feel free to take a look.'

The entire room, which must have been the full length of the house, had been converted into what looked like one of Burton and Fielding's squad rooms. There were filing cabinets and storage boxes stacked up around the perimeters, with a large table in the centre littered with papers, photographs and notebooks. In the far corner, a whiteboard not unlike their own corkboard, was filled with photos, writing and red string stretching from various sections to others. However, the most unusual feature was a life-sized cardboard cut-out of Burke, not dissimilar to the ones seen in bookstores during promotional events.

'I've been asked to write a book about my fascination with him,' Doris said walking up to the cut-out.

'How did it all start?' Fielding asked looking at the photographs on the table. Hannah joined her and started to go through the notebooks.

'It was my mother who got me interested. She's a huge crime fiction fan and recommended him to me. She even dragged me along to one of his book signings even though I was reluctant to go at the time. I found him to be very charming, which made me want to read his books. Over the years one thing led to another, and what you see around you now is the result.'

'This is fascinating,' Fielding said, moving from the table to the whiteboard. 'It must have taken you years to collect it all.'

'I started about ten years ago. A few clippings at first, but then it grew into the collection I have now. By the way,' she said, moving away from the figure and towards one of the filing cabinets, 'here's what you asked for.' She took the manila folder which had been left on top of it and handed it over to Burton. 'A full list of all the crimes in Jonas Burke's books, together with murders and protagonists. You can keep that: it's just a copy.'

Burton opened the file and quickly glanced through it. 'Has he ever mentioned anywhere, or even hinted at, who his police advisor is?'

'Not that I know of,' Doris admitted. 'He's very secretive about his sources so I hear.'

'Yes, that's what we've heard too.'

Now they had what they'd come for, Burton thanked the woman for her hospitality and the file and made a motion to the others that they should take their leave.

'There is one other thing,' Doris Mendelson said as she was standing at the door seeing them off, with her daughter comfortably nestled on her hip. 'Although Mr Burke keeps his public life and his private one very separate, I don't think that Jonas Burke is his real name.'

'What do you mean not his real name?' Hannah asked in surprise looking at the others.

'That's something else that he keeps tight-lipped about,' Doris confirmed, 'but I know for a fact that it's not the name he was born with.'

'How do you know that?' Burton asked, interested by her remark.

'He made a bit of a slip up once when giving a talk I attended. He tried to cover it up, and he did do a very good job of it, but not before I heard it and realised what he'd said.'

13

'Alan Bedlington didn't tell us that little gem about his name,' Burton said to the others when they were back in the car. Curtains and blinds twitched once again as he drove the car to the top of the cul-de-sac to turn it around.

'Perhaps he doesn't know?' Fielding raised the question though she had grave doubts that it was indeed the case.

'Perhaps he doesn't,' Hannah said from the back seat. 'If that's the case, Burke's been known by his pen name for so long now that he probably believes it to be true.'

'But you can't simply forget the name you were born with?'

'No you can't,' Hannah admitted, and she wasn't challenging that. 'It was just that an over-inflated sense of self may have taken over. I've done some psychology courses over the years, and I've seen it happen on a couple of occasions. Admittedly, it's unusual, but it isn't completely unknown.'

'Just something else to contend with,' Fielding murmured. They had enough to deal with without this little extra gem entering the equation. 'We need to speak to the man himself, don't we?'

Burton agreed. 'It looks that way, but let's see what we can glean from the information in this file first.'

Hannah had been overjoyed to meet Mr Jonas Burke the previous week, but all that had happened in the interim had changed her view of him. *You should never meet your idols*, she told herself, *as they really don't seem to live up to expectation.*

Over the next few hours they went through page after page of the file Doris Mendelson had prepared for them. Fielding had scanned all the sheets into the computer, and it was decided that rather than dividing them into three, one section for each of them to go through, they would all go over them so nothing would be missed.

'So what exactly are we looking for now?' Hannah had asked, mouse pointer already sitting on the file ready to begin.

Burton sat back in his chair. 'These are all descriptions of crime scenes – some fictional but, from what we know, there may be some being actual police records of real crime scenes also in there. In fact, we now know that it's more than a possibility. So if we can go through each in turn and cross reference with any cases from our database, then perhaps we can find out which police force they came from. We know already that one has come from the Northumbria Police records, but there may well be others. For all we know, Burke may have had other advisors in different police authorities, which would make this a bigger crime than already thought.'

'Good idea,' Hannah told him, clicking open the file. She was greatly disturbed by all this. If it were indeed true, and that a police officer – or police officers – had made Burke privy to real cases, then it had far larger implications. Burke began writing his bestsellers in 2003, so it was feasible that real cases had been used from then, even perhaps earlier.

However, regarding Doris Mendelson's revelation that Jonas Burke's name was not his real one, Burton needed to speak to the author personally about that. He pulled out his police note-book from his inside jacket pocket, and found the author's tele-phone number.

'It's not very convenient as I'm doing a book-signing in Sheffield tomorrow,' Burton was told by the author when he answered his phone.

Is he expecting some kind of leniency simply because he is a best-selling author? Burton thought that very arrogant of the man. But before the author had the chance to make any further objection, or try to obstruct their investigation, Burton simply told him that they would come down to see him. He heard the man let out a long impatient breath, but he too could play that game.

'If you'd rather we could always get a warrant for you to come into police headquarters up here tomorrow?' He said, and waited for the response.

'All right, all right,' Burke said, in a manner which showed his obvious annoyance. 'I'll be in Waterstones in Orchard Square shopping centre from 11am until two. But I have to say–'

'We'll see you there then.' And with that Burton put down the phone, relieving Burke of any more chances to protest or even finish his sentence.

'Nicely done!' Hannah beamed, and Burton bowed his head in thanks.

'Road trip again tomorrow then?' After a week of being confined to her mother's house, Sally Fielding and her partner had travelled more miles in one day than they normally did in about a month back home in Manchester. But she wasn't complaining. If all this led to finding the truth, then she didn't mind one little bit.

Another day, another journey. Setting off at just before 9.30am to avoid the early morning weekend shopping traffic, they reached Sheffield at around 12.30pm and parked up as near as they could to Waterstones. They'd certainly seen a lot of the country this week, taking in Cambridgeshire, Northumberland, and now Yorkshire.

Being a Saturday, Burton told Hannah that she needn't come along if she had family commitments, but she said that she'd like to. Everything now hinged on Burke telling them who his police advisor was, and if he wasn't willing to relieve himself of that information then Burton would get it out of him one way or another, and certainly wouldn't be shy in arresting him for withholding evidence – regardless of who the man thought he was.

Burton didn't like the man; he couldn't really say why, perhaps it was simply his overblown sense of importance. But Burton usually had a nose for these things and in his opinion there was something about him that just didn't sit right.

They had no difficulty finding Jonas Burke in the bookstore as there was a large pull-up banner heralding his position like an army standard at the rear of the store. *Nothing like flying your own flag*, Burton thought. On it was a photo of the cover of his book, his classic head-and-shoulder promo picture and his publisher's logo, a phoenix majestically rising skywards. Born out of the ashes of discarded submissions, the company had thrived since his joining it some sixteen years previously, going from a small indie brother and sister business into the huge international organisation it was today. Phoenix books was a highly reputable brand, and its logo was now recognisable worldwide. Both author and publisher had chosen one another well it seemed, and Burke's arrival and ultimate success had spawned thousands of other prospective crime writers submitting their manuscripts each year to the company in an attempt to gain a coveted contract with them.

A huge crowd was gathered around the table which had

been set up for him to sit at and sign copies of his latest offering for all his loyal and adoring fans. Burton and his team waited patiently as the line dwindled until, finally, there were no more left to pay homage to his greatness.

His smile on seeing them was more of a grimace disguised as a smile than a true one and it didn't go unnoticed by the detectives, especially by Burton who stood with his back up against one of the book shelves with his arms crossed. Then Burke caught sight of Hannah and recognition set in; at first he showed it by a slight grin which lifted one corner of his mouth, and then he pointed at her with one finger and the grin spread even further.

'Newcastle,' he said, rising from his seat, 'right?' When she nodded he came around the table and took her hand in his, kissing the back of it in a gallant, old-fashioned kind of way. He had annoyed her since she had started this investigation, but she felt a fluttering in the pit of her stomach. She could clearly see why he was so popular with his female fans: he was charm personified.

'Mr Burke!' Burton said. His voice was perhaps a little louder than he had intended, and it took the man by surprise.

'Yes,' he said equally sharply and let go of Hannah's hand to turn around to face him. 'You know ... DI Burton isn't it? ... I really can't tell you anything more than I've already told you.'

'Well I think that maybe you can.'

The author looked at him with a furrowed brow. What more could be wanted from him? He'd already given them the name of his researcher, who would doubtlessly be able to handle any queries they had. But this DI appeared to be the dogged type who would not be deterred by anything until he got the answer he wanted. Burke stood his ground, firm and resolute, with a jaw to match. 'This is bordering on harassment, detective,' Burke said sharply, 'and I repeat what I have just said. I have told you all I know ... which is essentially nothing.'

Burton reached into his jacket pocket and retrieved his police notebook. Undoing the elastic enclosure which kept all the pages tightly closed, he slowly flicked through until he found what he wanted. The man was going to play by his rules and not the other way around, which is why he deliberately took his time over it.

'Right,' he said finally finding what he could have easily found a few moments earlier. Burke was fuming, Burton knew it and he was loving it.

'We've had a chance to look through your researcher's notes and have noticed the letter W here and there in them.'

Burke shrugged his shoulders. 'So?' he asked, unsure where the detective was going with this.

'We were wondering,' Burton continued, as if uninterrupted, 'if that letter was your way of indicating that the information had been supplied by your police advisor?'

Burke looked at him incredulously. 'Is this what this is all about?' he asked spreading his arms wide. 'How am I supposed to know what a random letter is on the notes?'

Still calm, Burton simply asked, 'Well you put it on there, didn't you?'

'Me? No! I send handwritten notes now and again, but that's most likely down to the researcher and the advisor ... whoever that is!'

It was Fielding's turn to interrupt. 'What do you mean whoever that is? Surely you know who your own advisor in police matters is?'

'Actually, no, I don't, or didn't; Alan Bedlington's father did all of that for me. All of the notes you have were done by him and whoever his advisor was at the time he kept it to himself. Perhaps this letter W that you're going on about so much was his way of indicating that the information came from them. He accumulated a lot of data over the years prior to his death, one could almost say far too much, so much so that really all his son needs to do when I ask for any information is to go through all of it and pick out a few things for me to put in the book.'

That was not what Burton and his team wanted to hear, not by a long chalk. They were essentially now back to square one again.

'Am I free to go, detective?' Burke asked, but Burton had one last question. 'We need to know your real name, Mr Burke, and not just your nom-de-plume, so if you don't mind doing the honours.'

The author stared at him in shock. 'How on earth did–' he began, but stopped almost as soon as he started. He looked around for a piece of paper, finding one on the table where he'd been signing books, and bent over and wrote something down on it.

'That's the name and telephone number of my solicitor,' he said, thrusting it into Burton's hand. 'I suggest you contact him in future as I'm not prepared to answer any more of your questions.' Picking up his belongings from the table he bade them a reluctant good day, led from the scene by one of the bookstore's assistants who had been hovering nervously in the background throughout. They heard her apologising to him for this disturbance as they walked into the distance, and Burke looked over his shoulder at them and scowled before vanishing from sight.

Hannah Sanderson returned to her previous opinion of the man – but this time, rather than him simply being a bastard, she had extended her opinion of him to a complete and utter one.

14

'Well, that was a waste of time!' Fielding declared after he'd gone.

'Not really,' Burton disagreed with her, 'at least we now have the name and telephone number of his solicitor. If Burke's unwilling to play along with our questioning then I'm sure a brief call to,' he stopped and looked at the crumpled piece of paper in his hand, 'Mr Mark Bentley will advise him that he needs to co-operate fully with us.'

'Let's hope so,' she replied, but not sounding too convinced by it.

'Where to now then?' Hannah asked from behind them, and they spun around to see her. 'Back to HQ?'

'No, I think we'll call it a day for now and start afresh in the morning. Yes?'

The two women nodded agreeing with him, especially Fielding, as two consecutive days on the road was beginning to remind her of her trip on the continent – and that was something she didn't wish to be reminded of for a very long time to come.

By 9am the next morning they were back in North Tyneside and raring to go. Even though it was a Sunday, all three had willingly given up what was left of their weekend to go in and continue with the work. The job in hand was simple: cross reference every crime scene on Doris Mendelson's list with the police database and see what turned up. Three pairs of eyes were deemed to be better than one for this, just to make sure. The first case turned up in just over five minutes, and it was Hannah who found it.

'I've got one,' she declared, shocked at the speed of her own discovery.

Joe Burton leapt up from his seat, sending his chair flying backwards on its wheels with so much force that it hit the wall behind him and bounced back again, and went around behind her to look over her shoulder at the information she'd found.

'Me too,' Fielding echoed. Burton didn't know which way to turn, but stayed put for the time being.

As he quickly scanned Hannah's findings on the screen he saw that the case was the north east, at somewhere called The Angel of the North. Fielding had spoken to him about it before in derogatory terms (referring to it as a 'rust bucket', as he recalled) and it was a huge statue with what looked like wide outspread aeroplane wings. The body of a young girl had been found there one morning approximately eighteen months ago by an unsuspecting dog-walker. She had been strangled and then ornately tied to the base of the statue with her arms outspread to emulate the shape above her. The same scene had been in Burke's second from last book.

'Well done,' he said before moving on to see what Fielding had also turned up. Hers was perhaps a tad more gruesome. A body had been dismembered and packaged up into small bags in a supermarket freezer. The store manager had been made aware of it by a customer complaining of a strange smell coming from the frozen chicken section, and when he'd gone to investigate found something that he wished he hadn't. Beneath the top layer of goods he found a bottom layer of secreted body parts wrapped up in the store's own label plastic carrier bags. The customer swore blind that she'd heard him rather humorously say 'oh cluck' upon finding the cache, which she'd thought at the time to be rather insensitive given where they'd been found, but then it was later confirmed that she was slightly hard of hearing.

Unlike Hannah's finding, which had been in Gateshead, the body deposited in the freezer had been in a national supermarket chain in Malton, North Yorkshire. This delightful scene had taken place seven years ago and was captured for posterity in Mr Burke's new book, *Devilled*, and even included the infamously misheard 'oh cluck'.

'I just don't understand how these ended up as cold cases,' Fielding exclaimed. 'For example, that case with the body in the freezer. How could they have not seen who put the body parts in there? There are usually security cameras all around the inside of a supermarket, aren't there? Surely it wouldn't go unnoticed by somebody packing a freezer?'

'Unless they were a member of staff, that is,' Hannah observed.

'I agree,' Burton told Fielding. 'There are cameras all around supermarkets. Even if a member of staff had done it, Hannah, they too would have been caught on camera.'

'So how could that have ended up as a cold case?' Hannah was completely baffled.

'We need to find out who was on these cases at the time and recorded the information onto the databases, and then speak to them. In the meantime, though, let's continue and see how many more we can come up with.'

'This is not looking good,' Fielding said echoing all their thoughts.

Burton agreed with her. 'No, it's not looking good at all. But then, of course, there is another possibility–' he began, but Hannah's sudden utterance stopped him mid-sentence.

'Oh no, not another one!' she exclaimed loudly, eyes fixed on the monitor in front of her.

Burton started in surprise. 'What's wrong?' he asked, quickly leaving his seat again to see what she'd found.

She pointed at the screen, visibly shaken. 'This case...'

Burton followed her finger and quickly scanned what it read. 'I don't understand?' he said, shaking his head in ignorance as he looked at her. But Hannah was clearly disturbed by it.

'This was the first case I worked on when I joined the force in 1983,' she managed to tell him. 'Well, didn't work on exactly, but it was the first crime scene I attended. It even has the young constable's name as Johnstone – which was my maiden name!'

'What?' Burton spluttered.

'It describes the scene perfectly, far too perfectly in fact.'

'Are you sure, after all this time?' Although Fielding didn't doubt her, perhaps her mind was creating a false memory of actual events.

'I might be in my sixties, Sally, but that's not the kind of thing that you can easily forget. I remember getting a terrible blasting from the officer in charge because I threw up at the scene. Said I'd contaminated his crime scene, which admittedly I probably did, but he shouldn't have gone on at me to the extent that he did. I almost quit my job because of that day but my parents convinced me otherwise.'

'I can see how you'd remember it then,' Burton admitted. 'Think I would have too under the circumstances.'

He leaned over and read the whole thing again. 'It says here that there was a young boy in the house, hiding in a cupboard.'

'Yes, that's right, in the pantry,' Hannah confirmed, remembering the day as if it were yesterday. 'He was terrified, as I remember, but he said that he hadn't seen anything. I was in the room when the doctor examined him and he'd said that when his dad heard somebody trying to break in he told him to go and hide in there, which he did without hesitation. Said he stayed in there until the police came.'

'And he didn't see anything?' Burton asked somewhat astonished.

'No. He said that he was too frightened even to look out and just stayed in there throughout.'

'But he heard everything?' Sally asked and Hannah nodded.

'Poor boy,' Sally muttered, only imagining what he'd gone through.

'How does Burke end this particular story then?' Burton wondered if the similarity extended to the rest of what unfolded that day.

'I haven't read that far,' Hannah confessed as the discovery had stopped her going any further, 'but I don't know how all that ended myself as I was immediately moved on to another case before it was solved. That officer in charge was so determined to get rid of me that I never saw either him or his partner ever again.'

Burton thought the man sounded like a total bully. That sort of thing wouldn't happen these days, or at least he hoped it wouldn't. He looked again at the screen to see how Burke had ended his version of it, but the story had been left at the point Hannah had described, with the boy being taken out of the pantry to be seen by a medical examiner. As she'd said, described far too perfectly.

'I can only conclude from this that the person who provided Burke with the inside knowledge was one of those police officers. Don't you agree?' He looked questioningly at Fielding, and she couldn't fault his reasoning.

'What were their names, can you recall?' The question directed at Hannah.

'Oh yes,' she said defiantly, 'I'll never forget. DI Martin Scott and DS Barry Small. Their names have been etched in my brain since that day.'

'I'm assuming that they're now retired?'

'Oh I would think so, especially as I now am. Not sure how old they were when I had the dubious pleasure of meeting them but, looking back, perhaps not that much older than me. One thing for certain, though, they definitely weren't mature! It's a funny thing though, I can remember their names as clear as day, but I can't for the life of me remember the name of that young boy.'

15

Still stunned by Hannah's discovery, they finished checking all of Burke's notes and found twenty-five instances of crimes in his books matching those held on the national police database. The crimes had been committed not just in one area of the country but scattered all across it. There wasn't a pattern: these were just random acts of violence and destruction that left people dead or injured. But there was a common denominator: the perpetrator or perpetrators were never found, and they were now all cold cases.

'I'm really pleased that DCI Ambleton agreed to release you to Northumbria Police to help with this,' Fielding said to Burton as they were working. She and Hannah could have managed it themselves, but his extra pair of eyes and no-nonsense attitude were a blessing.

Burton had been dreading this conversation and wondering just how long it would be before it came up. 'Well... actually...' he began somewhat nervously, as he still didn't have his answer ready.

Fielding, of course, picked up on that. She had been partnered long enough with Joe Burton to recognise hesitancy when she saw it. 'What?' she asked, now suspecting that something was wrong.

'Well I am officially here,' he told her, shuffling a little uncomfortably in his seat. 'Ambleton contacted DCI Winters and confirmed that with him...' Burton's voice trailed off.

'And?' Fielding pushed for an answer. She saw Hannah wondering what on earth was going on but knowing not to get involved.

'I took holiday to come and be up here with you.'

The room fell silent for what seemed like an eternity, broken at last by Fielding's further questioning. 'But I thought that you said that it had all been arranged with our assistant chief constable in Manchester?'

'It was, I mean he did agree to it, but only if I came up here in an unofficial official capacity, if you get what I mean?'

Fielding wanted to know more, 'But why did he say that?'

'Hey, I don't know!' Burton was becoming frustrated by all of this, but more by the fact that he'd not told his partner the whole truth regarding his involvement with the case. 'Take that up with him. But let's just get past this and get on with the case, shall we?'

'Why did you take holiday? I still don't understand?'

'Because I wanted to help my partner!' The words thundered across the room. Then a little quieter, 'Because I wanted to help you find out what really happened to your father.'

Fielding got up from her chair and went around the desks to where Burton was sitting. Hannah sat and watched the scene play out, unsure of where it was going and thinking that she should perhaps leave the room; but she remained seated, primarily because the whole Burton–Fielding dynamic had her intrigued. Though she had worked closely with William Fielding, his daughter Sally was a stranger to her, and it was only in the past couple of days that she'd come to know her a little bit better. But never before had she seen two police officers so much in tune with each other. The events that were now playing out in front of her were, in her humble opinion, based on more than partner loyalty – and she knew a fair bit about that herself. But Joe and Sally, now their loyalty was something entirely different; there was more than mutual affection there, and she wondered if they even realised that they were in love with one another.

'Get up,' Fielding said and Burton obeyed. He'd expected a firm telling off so prepared himself for it. What he didn't expected, however, was her throwing her arms around him and giving him the biggest hug she'd ever given him – and probably anybody else for that matter. Finally releasing her hold on him she kissed him on the cheek and said 'Thank you' before going back to her seat. Hannah looked at Burton and smiled, and he returned the gesture.

If they know, then there's something definitely holding them back, Hannah thought. In her mind love strikes where it may, regardless of the kind of work you do, and she saw before her two people who should really be together on a more personal level.

'Right,' he announced after that little bit of drama had unfolded, 'let's get on with this then, shall we?'

After a list had been drawn up of the twenty-five crimes and their database file numbers, they grouped them into appropriate police authorities with the idea of contacting each in turn to speak to the officers who had been at the scene on the day and filled in the reports. They already knew who had attended the young boy's well-documented crime scene from Hannah's account – but they needed contact details for DI Martin Scott and DS Barry Small.

However, if any of the officers had leaked confidential information to Burke then the last thing they'd want to do was to admit it. Burton still wanted to confront them with it, though.

But that was for the next day: the majority of these officers would not be on duty with it being a Sunday.

'Let's call it a day,' he declared. The two women were happy to agree, although Hannah was noticeably disturbed that there were now two incidents she was personally involved with included in Burke's books. Half a day's rest was better than none, and they could start afresh in the morning, even if Fielding wanted to see this through to its conclusion as quickly as possible.

It was on the drive home that Hannah had a sudden revelation from the rear seat of the car. 'I know how we can find out what Jonas Burke's real name is,' she spouted out.

'How's that then?' Fielding turned around to face her, and the woman was bubbling with excitement.

'When I first met him at the book-signing in Newcastle I bought a copy of his book from him.'

'And?' Burton looked at her in his rear-view mirror.

'And,' she continued with enthusiasm, 'he handled the book himself when he inscribed it for me.'

'Of course!' Fielding was on the same page as her by now. 'His fingerprints must be all over it.'

Burton was overjoyed. 'Right then, bring your copy of the book in with you tomorrow and we'll get forensics to go over it. Let's hope that the man has his prints on file somewhere so we can find out exactly who he really is. If not, then it's going to have to be a talk with his solicitor, which I'm sure is not going to go down very well with either him or his client!'

They tried to relax for the rest of the day, but Burton and Fielding knew that the case was going to go round and round in their heads no matter how hard they tried to put it to bed for the night.

They were hopeful that Hannah's idea of Burke leaving his fingerprints on her book would bring back a result but then, as Burton had said, there was always the option of the solicitor to fall back on if that came to nothing. It was more than likely that a public figure such as Jonas Burke had not put a foot wrong in his life, which meant that nothing would come of any fingerprint search. However, there was always a chance that he might have strayed a bit in his younger years, and they couldn't let that opportunity pass.

When Fielding had called ahead and told her mother that they were returning earlier than expected, Mrs Fielding had gone out and bought all the necessaries for a Sunday roast dinner; something which delighted Joe Burton no end.

'I haven't had a proper roast dinner in years,' he told Sally's mother as they were all seated at the table later in the day.

'I used to have them all the time,' Mrs Fielding remembered, 'even mid-week on a Wednesday. Bill used to love his roasts, and so did Sally before she decided to turn vegetarian!'

'I still do,' her daughter reminded her, 'but only without the meat and gravy.'

'How can that even be a Sunday roast? Where's there a roast in that?' she exclaimed, laughing.

'Oh, Mum,' Sally chastised her and left the conversation at that, though she wanted to come back with 'roast potatoes' and fist pump the air. She cast a sideways glance at her partner: his smile suggested he was thoroughly enjoying the banter.

Complete carnivore, she thought to herself.

'Oh, by the way,' Mrs Fielding said as she was clearing the table after they'd eaten, 'something funny happened today.'

'What was that?' Sally asked her mother, joining her in the kitchen with some of the dishes.

'There was a white van sitting outside at the bottom of the drive for a long time. At first I thought that they were going to deliver something, but nobody got out of the van.'

'How long was it there?'

'It must have been a good hour or so. I even had to ask the driver if he could move so that I could get the car off the drive to go to the shops. He had one of those blue peaked caps on, and a padded jacket.'

'I'm sure it's nothing,' Sally reassured her mother, thinking how typical of a police officer's wife to notice the clothing details.

'Well it just looked a bit rude sitting outside somebody's house.'

'Oh, Mum, he was probably having his lunch or something,' Sally told her and began to wash the dishes.

'I do think he should have done that somewhere less public. It made me feel a bit uncomfortable actually, the two of them just sitting there all that time.'

'There were two people in the van?'

'Yes, a man and a woman.'

'Perhaps they needed two people if what was inside was too heavy for one person to lift?' Sally continued washing up, and thought no more of it.

16

The evening had been extremely pleasant – again Mrs Fielding was the perfect host – but the next morning brought home what was in store. When they went to pick Hannah up she was standing by the door waving Jonas Burke's book in the air to show them that she had it with her. Fortunately, being an ex-police officer, she'd had the foresight to put it into a clear plastic bag as to not contaminate it any further.

'Has anyone else held the book?' Burton asked as she made herself comfortable on the back seat.

'Me,' she said, 'and also the printers, the mailroom packers and staff in the bookshop.' They both knew they were hoping for the impossible: no fingerprints on record apart from Burke's, but knew that the odds were significantly stacked against it. In any case, it could take up to forty-eight hours for any results to come back to them from forensics, depending upon the backlog and importance of any requests in the queue before theirs. So for the time being they should concentrate all their efforts into speaking to the officers who handled those cases identical to the ones Burke had put in his books.

'It's just an odd thought,' Hannah said to Burton when he

returned from forensics, 'but how about mapping Burke's movements around the time of the deaths?'

'What are you thinking?' he asked her.

'It just occurred to me that he could have been in the area on one of his book signings and heard about a murder when he was there. Didn't you say that the researcher told you Burke was once a journalist? Perhaps he still knows people in the newspaper business who'd be happy to give him the lowdown?'

'But there's still the fact that he wrote details in his books that only the police would know about,' Fielding reminded her.

'Oh yes,' she reconsidered, feeling a bit deflated, 'there is that.' She thought that her idea had been a good one. How could Burke have known what was in an official report? There was no getting away from the conclusion that it had to be an inside job.

If that were the case then there would have to be an investigation regardless of how long ago it had happened. Police corruption was frowned upon at the highest level, whether in the present or in the past, and a serving police officer should certainly be seen to be above all of that. The implications were great, and very disturbing, but Burton was not going to shy away from them. If he found out that a fellow officer had betrayed his position for money, then he would be the first to point the finger of blame at them.

'How long did forensics say they would be with the testing?' Fielding asked.

'They couldn't promise anything,' he told her, 'but they said that they would see what they could do. I did mention the circumstances, so I hope somebody takes note of that and acts on it. At the worst, two days, by which time we should be well ahead with all the other work we have to do. Which means,' he continued, looking over to Hannah, 'that I think you should go ahead with your idea of seeing if any crimes were committed at the time Burke was having his book signings. Who knows: it might just bring something of value up.'

'I'll start on that right now,' she told him. The only way to do this was to contact the man's publisher to get a list of his book tour schedules. 'How far back should we go?' she asked Burton, looking for a point of origin to begin the search from.

'When did his books first come out?' he asked her, to which she replied 2004.

'Then I think you should start from there.'

Well you did suggest it! she told herself, and started what looked like a near-impossible task. It wasn't just a list of places he'd visited on book signings over the past fifteen years, it was also matching any crimes in those places on the same dates or as near to. Then, if that wasn't enough, she'd have to cross-check with the crimes as outlined in the researcher's notes. In fact ... she'd gone back to work again!

She'd just come off the phone to Burke's publishers with the promise of an email in due course giving her the full informa-tion she'd requested when there was a rap on the door. When it opened DCI Winters appeared from behind it.

'Just seeing how you're all doing,' he said, coming to a stop beside Burton's desk.

'Yes, everything is going fine,' the detective told him, looking up at the man now hovering over his shoulder.

'I'm heading upstairs to have a word with the chief constable as he wants to know how the case is going. Do we have anything concrete to tell him?'

Fielding was overjoyed that the chief constable was now involved in all this, and so he should be. Any hint of police corruption would have a devastating knock-on effect throughout the force at all levels. This was a very serious matter, and one which shouldn't be made light of. It had gone beyond investi-gating the circumstances surrounding her father's death.

Burton related to Winters everything they had found out so far and he listened with great interest before thanking them all for their continued work on the case.

'I'm sure the chief will be very interested to hear all of this. Keep up the good work, team.' And with that DCI Winters made a swift exit, heading to the 'big office', as he'd put it, on the top floor and leaving them to delve even deeper into what was turning out to be a very complicated case.

While Hannah was waiting for a response from the publishers regarding Burke's book-signing dates, she decided to look at Doris Mendelson's list of crimes in more detail. As she was now busily working on her own project, Burton split the twenty-five cases between him and his partner with him taking thirteen of them whilst giving Fielding twelve. It took less time than expected to discover who had been working on the cases.

However, they did notice something strange by the time the whole correlation had ended as an odd pattern had emerged. Reading through the notes it appeared that each of the twenty-five cases had been closed down with incredible haste. It was as if those involved had spent little time investigating and tracking down the killers.

'It looks deliberate,' said Burton. 'It's as if someone is controlling the outcome of the cases. When you look at them together, it sticks out like a sore thumb. But it might have gone unnoticed if each were looked at separately.'

'I don't like the look of this!' Fielding exclaimed, and Burton had to agree with her. 'It seems like a twenty-five-case cover-up.'

'But covering up what, that's the question. Is it corruption, or something else entirely?'

By this time Hannah had received the file and opened it, saving it to her desktop for easy access. She quickly read through the information and it was immediately apparent to her that there was a relationship between Burke's book signings and criminal activity. Whenever he had visited a city there had been a couple of unsolved cases on or around the same time. It didn't feel right. She was just about to mention it to her two team mates when there was another rap at the door.

DCI Winters had returned to let them know what the chief constable had told him. In light of what they had discovered, Chief Constable Malcolm had advised them to tread very carefully on this one and had given them until the end of the week to continue their investigation.

Burton was confused, as was Fielding. It sounded very much like a warning.

However, it was Hannah who voiced her thoughts on that statement. 'What exactly does he mean by that, Paul? Because surely if there has been an information breach, we need to find out who is responsible.'

Winters became very sheepish, shuffling his feet as if he didn't know quite how to respond.

'Paul?' Hannah pushed him for an answer. She and her late husband had known Paul Winters for a very long time. In her experience, he would not shirk from anything. So she was very confused by the ineffectual person she now saw standing before her.

'I'm sorry, Hannah, and you too, Detective Burton, Detective Fielding, but my hands are tied. What the chief constable says goes, I'm afraid, and if he says he's only going to allow you access to the files for the duration of the week then that's it. I'm sorry.'

'But why?' Hannah wasn't going to let this go in a hurry.

Winters repeated his apology and left the room, leaving the three stunned by what he had said. And it wasn't just what he'd said that disturbed them, but the manner in which he had said it.

'What the hell was all that about?' Burton asked Hannah as soon as the DCI closed the door behind him.

'I have absolutely no idea!' she exclaimed. 'I've known Paul Winters for my whole working life and he's never been one to turn away from a problem. I think he's been leaned on from above, which makes all this even more suspicious.'

'I agree,' Fielding told her. 'What is it that the chief constable doesn't want to find out? Because it's certainly looking as if he doesn't want us to get to the bottom of all this.'

'In that case I think we should work quickly,' Burton said. 'If we've only got until Friday to work here, then I say we find out as much as we can by then. If we don't, then we can carry on the investigation back in Manchester. Ambleton told us that she'd back us up on anything–'

'If Chief Constable Malcolm hasn't been in touch with her boss already.'

Burton turned to Fielding. 'What? You think that he would do that?'

'If we're getting too close to something, then I think that it's a distinct possibility.'

'Yes, but Ambleton wouldn't give up just like that, would she?'

'I'm hoping not,' Fielding told him.

'I think you've opened a can of very corrupt worms, Hannah,' Burton said, disturbed not only by this but by everything they had found out about in the past few days.

In the next few minutes things seemed to escalate very quickly. Firstly, Hannah's computer pinged, which indicated something had turned up on the alert that she had set up for crimes matching those in Burke's books.

'There are some historic crimes which match crimes in his earlier books,' she told them. But before anyone could speak her phone rang as well. As she very rarely got calls, and only then from her daughter Amy, she thought it best to check it. Excusing herself she delved in her bag to find her phone, which of course had to be right down in a bottom corner and, sure enough, Amy's photo and name were on the screen.

'I'd better take this,' she told her companions, and pressed the green answer button.

'Amy, what is it?' Hannah asked, as she'd certainly not been expecting a call from her. Nor had she been expecting the annoyance in her daughter's voice.

'Mum, why didn't you tell me you were redirecting a parcel to my address? It's just arrived now and you're lucky I was in!'

Hannah was confused. For one thing she hadn't ordered anything, and secondly, if she had ordered anything then she wouldn't redirect it to her daughter's house. If she knew that she wasn't going to be in, she'd have picked it up afterwards from the local collection office.

'Is there a return address?' she asked, now curious as to what it could be.

'Not that I can see,' Amy said. 'It only has your name on it as the addressee and then care of my address.'

'Just your address and not mine?'

'I just said that, Mum!'

From the exasperation in her daughter's voice Hannah realised Amy thought her mother wasn't paying attention. But Hannah wanted clarification of exactly what was on the package. You can't be a police officer all your life and not ask questions when they need to be asked. Since she didn't know what it could possibly be she asked her daughter to go ahead and open it.

'Just give me a minute then,' Amy told her, her voice trailing off as she said it. After a few moments she heard a blade slicing along the sealing tape then the rustle of packaging from within. 'I've no idea what this is–' Amy began, but then stopped suddenly.

'Are you still there?' Hannah asked after the line seemed to have gone dead. 'Amy?'

'I think you should come over and see this.'

'Why, what is it?' Hannah was worried by the sound of Amy's voice as her daughter wasn't normally ruffled by anything.

'And I think you should bring the two detectives with you.'

17

'A nd she didn't say what it was?' Burton asked when they were in the car and making their way to Hannah's daughter's house. He couldn't possibly see how the contents of the mystery parcel was related to the case, but he was certainly troubled by it.

'No, but she sounded shocked … and frightened,' Hannah told him, 'and she never gets frightened by anything. Plus, she insisted that we see it now, presumably before Millie gets back from school.'

Amy lived just a couple of streets away from her mother's house in Hebburn, and they could see her standing at the living room window looking out for them when they rounded the corner. She quickly disappeared only to reappear in the doorway as the car drew to a stop.

They all got out and Amy quickly ushered them into her home. She led them through to the kitchen where they saw a brown cardboard box sitting on the circular table. The flaps were open and pieces of shredded paper packaging were lying beside it. Some had even ended up on the floor and been left where they'd fallen. Amy stood back from it but indicated that they should take a look inside. As each edged closer and peered into the box they saw a smaller one within. It had likewise been opened but then, judging by the hurried telephone call to her mother, left for them to see.

Burton retrieved his pen from his inside jacket pocket and lifted back the flaps with it, careful not to actually touch anything which might have forensic evidence on it. Hannah looked towards her daughter who stood with her back towards the kitchen cabinets chewing on her thumbnail then back to the table again. What had she seen inside that had horrified her so much?

Fielding gasped when she saw what was inside. Looking up at her from the red-stained tissue paper was a pig's snout.

Burton turned around towards Amy and asked if she had a pair of tweezers he could use, and she quickly hurried off upstairs to find what he had requested. He had spotted a piece of paper with writing on it underneath the snout which he assumed was a note of some kind to them or, to be more precise, to Hannah. When Amy returned with the tweezers he managed to ease it out without either tearing or damaging it and he was right, it was a message, but it was written in what looked like German.

'How's your German?' he asked Fielding, hoping that on the off-chance she might be familiar with it. But she shook her head.

'I know German,' Amy offered. Her mother nodded, remembering that she'd studied it at A-level back in school along with English.

She leaned over and read it as Burton held it firmly between the tweezers.

'*Halt deine Nase raus, Schwein,*' she read, then exclaimed, 'oh!'

'What does it mean?' Burton asked her.

'It means,' she replied, 'keep your nose out, pig.'

Burton and Fielding exchanged glances. Then it was linked

in some way to what they were working on ... but how? And, more specifically, why was it addressed to Hannah Sanderson of all people and not them? And why was it in German?

'What can you tell me about either the delivery van or the driver, Amy?' Burton asked Hannah's daughter.

'"Nondescript" is probably the best way I can describe him,' she told him. 'I didn't pay that much attention to tell the truth. Who does?'

Burton knew exactly what she meant. Somebody knocks on the door, you get a parcel you may or may not be expecting, you sign for it ... wait. 'Did you have to sign for it?' he asked her, hoping that the answer would be yes. At least that might be some sort of a clue. If it was a business delivery then perhaps the van had an insignia on it or had markings of another kind, something they would be able to trace.

Amy stood and thought then answered in the negative. 'I didn't, come to think of it; it was just an ordinary, plain van with nothing written on it.'

'Big or small?'

'Small,' she told him, 'a small white transit. As for him, he was wearing a cap with a peak and a padded jacket.'

Before Burton could ask any more questions Fielding interrupted him. 'A white van, you say?'

Amy nodded.

'And he was wearing a cap with a peak and a padded jacket?'

'Yes. One of those baseball-type caps. Blue, as I recall.'

Fielding looked at Burton, and he acknowledged what she was referring to. The van and its driver seemed identical to the one which had been outside her mother's house. The description of both was exact, right down to the colour of the cap he was wearing. This was too much of a coincidence for them to ignore.

'Was there any sort of logo you could see on the jacket?' Burton continued.

'No, nothing. I'm sorry, detective, but there was absolutely nothing to say where he was from. My mother asked me about a return address and, again, there was nothing, just the typed label with her name, care of my address on. I just thought ... well, I thought that it had been redirected, which is why I rang. It's a miracle that I'm even here today; I had a doctor's appointment this morning and had only been back in the house a few moments before it was delivered.'

'We'll have to get this back to the police headquarters and get forensics to take a look at it,' he told Fielding and she agreed.

'Do you have any rubber gloves?' Burton asked Amy, who said that she had and went away in search of a pair. Neither had thought to pick up a pair of nitrile ones on their way out as, quite frankly, they hadn't known what to expect. Speaking of which, when Amy returned with a pair of very unusual Marigolds Burton didn't react, but kept his cool and asked her if the delivery man had worn gloves. She thought about it then replied that no, he had not.

'Good,' he told her, 'if he's on record then we should be able to track him from his prints.'

'And if he isn't?' she asked him. 'Because I don't fancy him turning up here again and my daughter answering the door.'

'Let's for the moment hope that he is, but if he isn't, we'll have to try and track down his van by other means. At exactly what time did he deliver this, can you remember?'

'Why yes, it was at about five to ten.'

'You thinking about CCTV?' Fielding asked him, as that's the way she would have gone about it if there was nothing else to go on.

'Yes, that's exactly what I'm thinking.'

But before leaving Burton had one last question to ask Hannah's daughter. 'Does your daughter have any printing ink?'

Amy looked a bit confused by the question, but told him that she did.

'In that case,' he said to her, 'could you please get it for me, and a sheet of plain white paper too if you have it.'

While Amy headed off upstairs to look for the items Burton had requested, both Hannah and Fielding knew where he was going with this.

'Well it's pointless to drag her all the way into police head-quarters just to take her prints then bring her back again; this will do the trick just as well.'

Fielding agreed. 'At least forensics will be able to eliminate her prints from the package.'

When Amy returned with paper and pad in hand, Burton told her what he was going to do and asked if she was happy with it. 'This will, of course, be destroyed as soon as forensics have compared them to the prints you must have left on the box.'

As Amy sat at the table the thumb and fingers of both her hands were individually pressed on the black ink pad and then onto the paper, giving a perfect copy of her prints. She smiled up at her mother. 'This reminds me of the time when I was little and Dad did exactly the same thing to show me what he did at work!'

Hannah laughed. 'Yes, I remember that as well, and I also remember how he said to get it off ... alcohol! I couldn't stop laughing when he brought out the bottle of vodka!'

Now finished, Burton carefully lifted the sheet of paper with the German writing on it using the rubber gloves he'd put on himself and slipped it inside the box for safekeeping. Fielding suppressed a laugh as the sight of him wearing them was some-thing to behold. They couldn't have been just ordinary rubber gloves, they had to be a pair of novelty ones. She'd seen his look of disbelief when Amy had handed them to him, followed closely by embarrassment. It must have been going through his mind at that point that he'd be taking the box into police head-quarters with them on his hands. Each of the pink gloves had a white boa and pearl trim at the cuff, with a costume jewellery ring on the third finger of the left hand. If the situation hadn't been so serious Fielding would have howled with laughter.

18

When they arrived back at police headquarters Burton immediately took the box up to DCI Winters's office. The DCI briefly looked inside at the contents then called for one of the forensic team to come and collect it straight away. Burton was more than happy to remove the novelty gloves lent to him by Hannah Sanderson's daughter. Winters looked quizzically at them but didn't ask ... and Burton didn't tell.

Burton had considered not saying anything about the tight deadline the chief constable had put on their investigation. But he felt obliged to mention it to Winters. He didn't feel right about just leaving it. 'Look, sir,' he began, 'I realise that your hands are tied, but we're going to do our damnedest to get through as much as we can before Friday.'

'I appreciate that,' said Winters, 'and you're right, my hands are tied. I feel that I'm stuck in the middle here and it's not the way I want it to go. I'm not really sure why the chief constable has decided to give you only until Friday, but he must have had his reasons. You can understand that, can't you?'

Burton nodded, even though it grieved him to do so. In his

mind, the only reason the chief constable would have given them a deadline would be to speed the enquiry along – not that they needed it as all of his team wanted it resolved as soon as possible. It was very personal for two of them, and for him too if it came to that as it involved the death of his partner's father. This was an extremely serious matter that needed to be investigated and resolved in the shortest time possible.

'Is Hannah all right, though?' Winters asked.

'Better than her daughter I would say,' Burton admitted, remembering Amy's reaction to the package. 'She took it pretty badly, which is understandable given that she has a young child in the house, albeit she was at school at the time. Which makes this all the more suspicious as Amy said that she shouldn't have been at home, and had only taken time off work for a doctor's appointment.'

'So you think that this has something to do with the case?' Winters asked.

'If it hasn't then I don't know what else it could be to do with, do you?' Burton asked and Winters shook his head.

Burton didn't want to mention that what looked like the same white van and driver had been spotted outside Fielding's mother's house, even though that troubled him as much as Amy's encounter.

'Hannah has worked for the police force for as long as I can remember, prior to her very recent retirement that is, and nothing like this has ever happened to her before. I mean, back in the early days she and most of the other female recruits had problems with some of the male chauvinists, especially as she continually beat them for promotion, but I seriously can't believe any of them would hold a grudge for that long. Or at least I hope not; not enough to do this.' He made a hand gesture towards the box on his desk.

'It means that somebody knows her and knows her family,

and their home addresses, so I'm a little concerned what they would do next, never mind what the motive is.'

'To put her off the case you mean?' Winters suggested.

Burton couldn't resist his next comment. 'You mean like the chief constable has tried to put us off?'

'No, I don't think he's trying to put you off; it's most likely politics.'

'But wouldn't you think that he'd want to follow this line of enquiry through to the end?'

'Yes, of course I do,' Winters told him, 'but I don't know who he's got on his back.'

They both fell silent, neither wishing to end up in an argument with the other.

'But why Hannah?' Burton eventually broke the silence. 'Why try to put her off, because from what I've already seen of Hannah Sanderson in the few days that I've known her, she doesn't seem the type of person who would be put off by anything or anyone?'

'But it's a bit different when somebody's family is dragged into it as well.' Winters's point was a valid one, Burton thought. *It's all very well targeting somebody because they are working on a case, but then targeting their family too ... well, that is an entirely different matter.* And the van outside Mrs Fielding's home; was that a threat too?

'Just try to get as far as you can with this by Friday, for all our sakes. I'm not happy with this either, you know,' Winters told him, and Burton thanked him for that.

After a member of the forensic team had taken the box away Burton returned to his office to join the others. When he opened the door Fielding was standing behind Hannah and they were looking intently at the monitor.

'Come and look at this,' Fielding said excitedly, waving him over to see what they'd found.

'What is it?' he asked.

Hannah took over. 'As you may recall my computer pinged just about the same time my daughter rang me so I didn't get a chance to look at it properly. There's another historic crime which bears a striking resemblance to one in Burke's earlier books.'

'Yes, but this one's a bit different,' Fielding told him.

Burton was curious. 'In what way?' he asked.

'This one had a piece of paper fastened to the man's shirt with a safety pin with the letter W inscribed on it.'

You know that he's working hard to get this done; he's even recruited people now to do his bidding.

People from his past, he says. He tells you that he can easily find them; he knows how to use his investigation and research skills.

He has easy access to all those things now, to throw them off the scent.

They're getting closer, and they have to be stopped.

'What?' Burton was stunned, as was Fielding. 'A W written on it? Does it mention the letter in Burke's book?' he asked Hannah, trying to get his mind around all of this.

'It doesn't. It mentions a piece of paper being attached to the shirt, but there's nothing written on it. In Burke's book it says that whatever was on was washed off when the body was left out in the rain, but the rest of the description is exact.'

'Wait a minute,' Fielding said, joining the conversation and leaning in towards the screen. 'Can you close in on that piece of paper for a minute, Hannah?'

'What are you seeing?' Burton realised that she must have seen something that they hadn't. Once Hannah had enlarged the photograph as much as she could without losing its definition, Fielding pointed to the monitor.

'There, can you see it?' As her index finger rested on the image they saw what she was indicating. The W wasn't actually the letter W, but it was in fact two Vs positioned very closely together. They were easier to make out once the picture had been enlarged, and could easily have been mistaken for a letter W.

'Well spotted,' Burton told her, proud of his partner's observational skills; but then had another immediate and more worrying thought. 'What if all the Ws we've been seeing on the researcher's notes aren't Ws at all, but are, in fact, two Vs like this?'

Fielding considered. 'I suppose they could be.'

'But this has only made things more difficult,' Hannah told them. 'We had no idea what the letter W meant, so how can we hope to know what two Vs might be?'

Burton ran a hand through his hair. 'This is turning into one hell of a puzzle!' he exclaimed, looking at both Hannah and Fielding in turn. Returning to his desk he slumped down in his chair and spun it around to face the window, staring out into the space beyond. He didn't know what to make of all this. Firstly, a bestselling crime author somehow siphons crimes from the police databases, and then research notes have the letter W ... correction, now two letter Vs ... scribbled onto them. The only people, other than themselves, to know about the letter business were Alan Bedlington and DCI Paul Winters. There was also the incident of the box delivered to Hannah via her daughter's address. That was sent as some kind of message if the German translation was anything to go by. And there was another thing –

why the German writing; what on earth did it all have to do with Germany?

But what did it all mean? Was there police corruption involved in leaking the documents, and if so, why? Was it for money, as that was all he could think it was for? Somebody somewhere was hiding something, somebody high up perhaps, but he as sure as hell was going to find out who it was. What started out as a personal investigation into his partner's father's death had now turned into something more serious … and sinister.

It was Fielding who broke the silence, bringing Burton out of his deep thoughts. 'Should I get to work on the CCTV around Amy's street?'

'Yes, that's a good idea,' he told her, rising from his seat and picking up his mobile phone from the desk. 'You start on that and I'll jump in as well when I get back; I've just got to go out and make a quick phone call.'

'You can make it here…' Fielding began, but he was already out of the door before she could finish her sentence.

He didn't want either her or Hannah to hear his phone call to DCI Ambleton as this was something that he needed to be on his own to do. He had something very important to ask her to do and which might conceivably throw a different perspective on to the case, so he needed it to be between him and her, and only him and her.

'Hello, Joe, how's it going up there?' His boss, and long-standing friend, asked him when she answered his call.

He let out a long exhale. 'Well, it's proving to be something a little bigger than first thought,' he told her honestly.

'Oh, in what way?'

He told her what they had so far. She listened with interest as he went through every aspect of the case before finally asking her the question.

'Are you sure?' Ambleton asked in astonishment.

'Not 100 per cent, in fact, not at all,' he admitted, 'but I think that it's an avenue I need to explore.'

There was a long pause before she replied. 'Well, you know I trust your judgement, Joe, always have done, so I can make some very discreet enquiries for you and come back to you with what I find out. But, I have to say, I honestly don't know who is going to have the answer to this.'

'I know, I know, and I'm sorry that I have to ask this, but my gut feeling tells me that I have to pursue it.'

'Okay, that's good enough for me.' Burton knew that Ambleton and Fielding were very much alike – both were dogged and relentless when the need arose – and at that moment he needed, no relied upon, his boss being just that. He went back to the office to await her call, which would tell him if what he suspected may actually be the case.

19

The CCTV footage showed a white van travelling east on Argyle Street and heading towards Jarrow town centre. It parked up and remained stationary in the car park of Palmer Community Hospital.

By zooming in on the van's registration plate they could get a good, clear picture of what it read. *Success*, thought Burton and got to work on tracing who the van belonged to. As the whole process only took a matter of minutes, he should have realised that things couldn't possibly have been that simple. He located the information, but when he read the make of vehicle the registration revealed, he uttered a disappointed 'Oh!'

Fielding knew that it wasn't a good sign.

'Well that's a dead end then,' he continued, and went on to tell them that the plate was officially registered to an Angela Fairbanks and the vehicle was not a white van as hoped for, but for a Fiat Panda.

'Has the car been reported missing?' Hannah asked, feeling certain that the car must have been stolen and the plates used to cover the van's own.

Burton quickly scanned another database but the answer

was no. 'Just somebody picking a random number plate and then making a copy of it, I guess,' he told her, feeling deflated.

'But it's a lead,' Fielding offered, 'and it's the only one we've got at the moment so I think that it might be worth going to see her, don't you?'

'Like you say, it's a lead,' Burton agreed with her and jumped up, grabbing his coat from the back of his chair. 'Another road trip anyone?'

As luck would have it Angela Fairbanks lived not too far from their current location in North Tyneside in a pleasant semi-detached house not too far from the DFDS Seaways ferry terminal and the Royal Quays shopping outlet centre, which meant that they only had a short drive to go and see her.

'I must come here one day with Amy,' Hannah had said more to herself than anyone else in the car as they passed the signs for the shopping centre. She'd mention it to her when she got home, and perhaps her choosy young granddaughter could finally decide upon something that she actually liked for the wedding so that they could buy it for her.

Angela Fairbanks wondered what on earth the police could possibly want to speak to her about as she invited them all into her home.

'Well that's not my car!' she exclaimed when Burton had shown her the photograph of the van with her own car's registration plates on it. 'As you can see,' she told them, pointing out of the window to her yellow Panda on the driveway, 'that's my car out there. I don't own a van, and never have; someone must have copied my plates.' Then as an afterthought, 'Can people actually do that, copy your plates and then stick them on another vehicle?' The woman looked horrified. Had they been used in a robbery maybe, a hit and run, carrying stolen goods, drug-running, a murder? Her mind was running away with her, frightened as to what they may have been used for.

'Do you know anyone who owns a van like the one in the picture?' Fielding asked her, but again she repeated her previous statement with the addition of no, she did not know anyone.

'Look, I'm sorry but I can't help you,' she said, still distressed, 'but as you can see, my car is out there, and the plates in your photo obviously don't belong on that van, so it looks as if someone has used them to hide whatever it was they were doing.'

Another dead end, Burton decided, so there was nothing more they could do here. The van driver had obviously had duplicate plates made, very likely randomly chosen, so Ms Fairbanks looked to be an innocent victim in all this. So they thanked her for all her help, apologised for disturbing her, and took their leave.

'Will I be in trouble for somebody using my plates?' Angela asked them as she stood at the door after seeing them out.

Burton reassured her that they would record the incident as a case of stolen number plates, so there would be no comeback on her.

'Do we trust her?' Fielding asked Burton when they were in the car and heading back to the office.

'I don't see why not,' he told Fielding. 'Her reaction seemed genuine enough, but we could drive past the house later this evening just to see if a white van is hanging around ... just to be sure. I think as well, if you're okay with it, we'll ask your mother about the white van that was outside the house.'

'What white van outside Sally's mother's house?' Hannah hadn't been told about the van parked on the road beside Mrs Fielding's property.

'Mum said that there was a van just sitting there for an hour on Sunday morning, and she had to ask the driver to move so she could get the car off the drive.'

'So she would have seen him?'

'Yes, she even described what he was wearing, and it was identical to how Amy described the man who left the parcel at her house.'

'We could do with a photo fit,' Burton stated. 'Although we don't want your mother to worry unduly, Sally.'

'Perhaps we could tell her that it's some kind of scam; someone pretending to be a delivery driver, and that we're warning people to be cautious by distributing an image of the person.'

'Good idea,' he told her, 'and you're not wrong as it looks like someone is pretending to be a delivery driver.'

20

When they arrived back at the office DCI Winters was waiting for them, and it looked suspiciously as if he'd been going through all their findings. Burton was concerned, especially after the conversation he'd only recently had with the DCI.

'You've done some good work here,' he said, closing a file and rising to vacate the desk for them, 'all of you.'

'We've still got a long way to go before Friday, sir,' Burton told him, adding a dig about the end of week deadline. They'd barely touched the surface of their investigations and now there was the incident with the parcel addressed to Hannah to deal with. It had to be linked, but in what way? Plus, Burton and his team had agreed to keep the majority of their findings to themselves, only going to Winters as and when necessary and for something that would be of assistance to them.

'We need to get something back from forensics,' Burton said, slumping down in his chair after Winters had left.

Forensics would be at least another day in lifting fingerprints or DNA from the package containing the pig's snout. That left the twenty-five crime cases over five police authorities to look into. There were five from each of the following: Avon and Somerset Constabulary, Cleveland Police, Northumbria Police, Sussex Police, and Wiltshire Police; far too deliberate to ignore as there was a definite pattern and a regularity to it. The only irregular thing was the timeframe, as the crimes had been spread over Burke's sixteen-year writing history.

The room was silent for quite some time as they were busily compiling a list of all the officers who had handled the cases in each of the five authorities. But by the time Burton had compiled his and moved on to the second batch he saw something which made him halt. He double-checked it, but there was no disputing what he was seeing there in black and white in front of him. One batch of five with the discrepancy was strange enough, but to find another one ... well, that was way beyond coincidence.

'Come and look at this,' he said. Fielding and Hannah came around behind him. He pointed to the printout on his desk and then to the computer screen, index finger resting on the first name on the crime report.

Fielding and Hannah both felt a chill run down their spines. Neither needed to look at Burton's list to see the connection; they both had a similar list ready to be printed out on their own computers.

'I don't get it–' Hannah began looking at the screen and then down to his list on paper.

'The printout is from Northumbria Police,' Burton told her, 'and the one on the screen is Avon and Somerset.'

'But I have that too,' Fielding told him, 'only it's from another force.

'Same here,' Hannah also said, 'mine's Cleveland.'

'But that's impossible!' Fielding declared.

'Yet here it is.' Burton scratched his head and leaned back in his chair as far as it would allow him to go without him falling backwards onto the floor. 'I don't like the look of this one little bit.'

When they checked the remaining police force, they found the same results. In every one of the five authorities, the same officer had signed off each case within a day or two of it being opened, thereby making them essentially cold cases as the perpetrator of the crime in question had not been found. It would have been unusual if this had only happened in one of the five authorities, but for it to happen in all of them simply wasn't coincidence – it was something far more sinister. Even a layman would see this as a 99.9 per cent impossibility.

It only meant one thing, and it was something that they would have been loath to admit had they not seen the evidence for themselves. How could one person sign off on cases in five separate police forces? The simple answer was, they couldn't. This case had moved a long way from simply investigating the circumstances surrounding the death of Sally Fielding's father. Now it reeked of corruption. And they only had until the end of the week to solve it.

'Surely the chief constable will change his mind when he sees this evidence?' Hannah couldn't believe that he wouldn't. 'If I hadn't bought that book we would have never known anything about all of this.'

'Unless he doesn't want to,' Burton announced.

The two women turned to face him. 'Think about it,' he continued. 'We're discovering things that were intended to be kept under lock and key. What if he knows about it and is covering it up, and making sure that we don't find out the truth?'

'But why? I just don't understand,' Hannah frantically asked. 'Surely it's not all about being bribed to keep it quiet; I just can't imagine our own chief constable capable of doing something like that!'

'Anyone is capable, Hannah, with the right incentive.' Burton felt sick to his stomach. He loved the police force and all it stood for, and he was proud to be a member of it, but this just seemed to be an abuse of that revered position. He righted his chair and reached for his phone, announcing that he was going to ring his boss, DCI Ambleton in Manchester.

'What about DCI Winters?' Hannah asked him.

'Hannah, I know that he's an old friend of yours, but I'm not entirely sure that we can fully trust him. I mean, with the letter W: as far as we know that could refer to him, with the W standing for Winters.'

It was like a slap in the face for Hannah. She'd known Paul Winters for many, many years; surely he couldn't be involved in something like this, could he? She fell silent, and it wasn't unnoticed by either Burton or Fielding.

'Look, Hannah,' Fielding tried to make the moment a little easier for her, 'Joe is right, we can't be sure about anyone. There are several people who know we are investigating Jonas Burke, and DCI Paul Winters is one of them. The sooner we make progress with the investigation the sooner we can clear his name.'

'Yes,' she muttered, 'I know that you're right, but I just can't believe–'

'I know, me too.'

To trace the person who had signed off on all the cold cases, Burton keyed the police officer's name into the force's database and was very surprised by what it turned up.

DCI Elizabeth Ambleton listened intently to what Burton had to tell her, and she wasn't pleased one little bit. 'I have no words!' she eventually told him when he'd finished. 'And with all this evidence you've been given a Friday deadline? Of course you must delve into this as far as you need to and you have my complete support on any line of questioning you need to take, no matter how high you have to go up the food chain. When we end this conversation I'm going upstairs to have a word with the chief constable and ask him to speak to his counterpart up there. Also, we can't have you looking into this while taking holidays, so I'll be insisting that all this semi-unofficial attendance be scrapped and that you should be heading up an official enquiry into what's looking like police corruption.'

'Thank you, boss.' He'd have been happy to do all of this as holiday, but, as Ambleton said, this was turning into a long and drawn-out enquiry that demanded both his and Fielding's full attention. If Northumbria Police's chief constable still insisted that they stop their enquiries in a few days, he and Fielding would go back to Manchester and work on it from there.

'So is Fielding officially back to work as well?'

'She is,' Ambleton confirmed, 'I've already sorted the paperwork out with the necessary department, so she has been officially back since the first day you started on this enquiry.'

'I'll tell her.' And with that Ambleton ended the call. Burton could only imagine how the conversation would go with the chief constable, and he didn't envy what the man would be obliged to do next. An enquiry into the integrity of any police force's officers was not one that any chief constable wanted to partake in but, sadly, this now seemed to be inevitable. What started off as something relatively simple had turned into something quite heinous.

21

'So who is DS Koder?' DCI Winters asked, looking at the five lists laid out on his desk.

Burton and his team had discovered that the twenty-five cases in the five different police authorities had been over-seen by a DS Koder, and he or she had speedily signed off the cases as unsolved. As the likelihood of this was astronomically impossible, Burton felt that they had no other option but to report their findings to DCI Winters, regardless of his growing suspicions about the man and those above him. He had asked them for any updates, specifying that nothing was too small, so that's what they would do, as long as they did not give too much away. What they'd now found could hardly be classified as small, but Burton felt that anything said to him should be handled with a fair degree of caution.

'That's just the thing,' Burton responded to Winters's question. 'DS Koder doesn't exist; there's never been a DS Koder serving in any force.'

'But somebody must have worked on the case: at least one person but more than likely two and their team, so I don't understand how this could have even happened?'

'There's only one answer, Paul,' Hannah quickly responded to her former colleague's question, acting as spokesperson and voicing what the other two were thinking. 'I'm now connected, it seems, to two of Burke's documented crime scenes, and can say categorically that nobody on the team I worked with was named Koder. These entries have all been doctored.'

It was something that nobody wanted to admit, but there was no other answer as all the evidence in front of them clearly pointed to that fact.

Winters reached across for the phone on his desk and keyed in four numbers. While waiting for an answer he cupped his hand over the mouthpiece and told the trio across the desk from him that he was going to get digital forensics to go over the files. 'If anybody can get to the bottom of this then they can; I'll ask them to extract and dissect all the files signed by this DS Koder.'

After thanking him, Burton and his team left the office. He was still highly suspicious of Winters, but the man seemed to be doing all that he could to help them, which perplexed Burton even more. By the time they reached their own office he had made a decision.

'Right, while forensics are working on that I suggest we get in touch with Jonas Burke's solicitor to find out what the man's real name is.'

The others agreed with him. Burke had to be the key figure in this; how else could he have obtained the information featured in his bestselling books other than through document leakage? The degree to which he was involved was something that they had to determine. Even if he wasn't personally responsible for it, he could have hired others to do it on his behalf, and that was something they could charge him for.

Burton rifled around in his jacket for his book but couldn't find it. 'Hey, have you seen my–' he began, but then spotted it behind the telephone. *Funny, I don't remember taking it out of my pocket today*. But, he thought, with all that had happened maybe he had and simply overlooked it. Flicking through the pages he found the solicitor's telephone number and dialled.

'This is harassment–' Mark Bentley began, but Burton immediately put him in his place by stating that his client was now required to help them with a criminal incident.

'What criminal incident?' The solicitor retorted, to which the detective responded that it was in connection with the release of sensitive information.

'Okay then,' Bentley replied.

But to Burton that result had come too easily. The lack of challenge disturbed Burton. The man appeared to have backed down without an argument – which was not how he'd imagined the conversation would go. Had Bentley been expecting the call? It seemed like he'd been prepared for it. Burton had never hidden his dislike of solicitors, having clashed horns with them on more times than he cared to even think about. They always seemed to have a ready answer for everything and would try their hardest to thwart the police. But this one, Mark Bentley, he seemed to know what was coming, and also what he was going to be asked.

'On one condition, though,' the solicitor added.

Burton thought, *Here we go*. 'And what is that, Mr Bentley?'

'You'll need a court order, and I'll also have to speak to a couple of people first before I can talk to you further about this.'

Although annoyed by the man and his delaying tactics, Burton felt he had to agree, but not before reminding Bentley that this was a serious matter and not to be taken lightly by either him or his client.

The solicitor said that he understood.

Burton sincerely hoped that he did. If this was the only way they'd get to the truth then so be it. And he went about setting wheels in motion for the court order.

22

Sally Fielding was pleased to hear that she was officially back at work, and had been since the beginning of this case.

It seemed odd to call it a case when she was investigating the circumstances surrounding her own father's death, but perhaps this was necessary to impersonalise it for her. Not everyone had what she begrudgingly called the luxury to look into a family member's death. But now given this opportunity she would handle it in a professional manner until there was a satisfactory resolution and those responsible were held to justice.

'So, how do you feel about officially being back to work then?' Burton asked after giving her the news.

'Yes, it feels good, but I would have gladly done it on my own time.'

'I know you would have, but at least this way it's official.'

'You know, I've been thinking,' she continued, 'I've been putting it off, but I really feel I have to tell my mother about what we're doing. I was going to wait until the case had finished, but now I'm not so sure about that. What do you think; you know I value your judgement?'

Before Burton could respond, an email pinged into his inbox. In fact, the same thing happened to each of the three computers almost simultaneously. Excusing himself, he went over to his desk and opened it, and as he did a video popped up onto the screen and began playing without him having to do anything to make it start.

'What the–' he began, staring at the dimly lit screen, moving in closer to the monitor to try to see what it was. It was hard to make out what was playing on the video at first as it appeared to be filmed in near darkness, but then he saw the shaky hand-held camera move over towards two plastic chairs. Two figures were sitting on them, and if the back view of long hair hanging down was anything to go by, each appeared to be young girls. They were sitting motionless and were tied to the chair with a thick nautical rope encircling their bodies securing them to the seat. *What was this? what was happening?*

'Joe, what's going on?' He heard Fielding's voice and then Hannah's asking a similar question before a voice spoke from the video, disguised by a distorting device.

'These two girls are sitting here very quietly and behaving themselves. Now why can't you three do the same?' It was a menacing tone, and although not mentioning them by name, it was definitely directed to the three of them watching it. 'Now Jemima and Millie, smile for the camera!'

Hannah let out a gasp before reaching into her bag for her phone. However, as the camera moved around to the front of the girls it revealed them both to be mannequins.

'Next time,' the voice continued, 'they will be the real thing.' The video ended abruptly. Hannah's phone dropped to the desk with a thud as they continued staring at their screens in total disbelief at what they'd just witnessed.

'What in the hell was that?' Burton's voice was frantic. Apart from the fact that the video was directed specifically at them, the person in the recording led them to believe that the two 'children' were Doris Mendelson's daughter Jemima, and Hannah's granddaughter Millie. He checked his mailbox to play it again but the email had vanished from the system.

'We need digital forensics down here, and fast!' he snarled, still looking at the space on the screen where the video should have been.

Fielding was on it straight away and snatched her phone from its cradle. She had no idea which extension they were on so simply pressed zero hoping that somebody would be at the other end of it like they were in Manchester. She hurriedly asked for digital forensics and was put through to somebody called Lex Barker. As Lex turned out to be female, Fielding presumed that it was a shortened version of Alexis. After Fielding had explained the situation, Ms Barker told her that she would be along to see her immediately and asked for her room number. As that wasn't something that Fielding had paid much attention to she had to excuse herself while she went to look.

'We're just in this office as a temporary measure,' she felt obliged to tell the girl after giving her its number and location. It seemed silly to tell someone that she didn't actually know where she was. Lex laughed softly telling her not to worry, promising to be over within the next ten minutes.

Digital forensic analyst Lex Barker knocked on their door long before the ten minutes had passed. If you had asked Fielding to describe the person coming along to see them she would most definitely have been way off the mark. She certainly couldn't have envisaged a petite, spiky-haired, punk-like young girl with a penchant for dark clothing, who reminded her a lot of Lisbeth Salander from *The Girl with the Dragon Tattoo*, only Lex did not sport any facial piercings.

Hannah was a bit shocked, as her outfit was hardly police

regulation, but Burton was unperturbed. He invited Lex to take a seat and briefly took her through the circumstances. He knew that Fielding had already briefed her up to a point, but he wanted to fill her in with a bit more information.

'You must have really pissed someone off!' Lex declared after hearing him out.

'It's starting to look that way,' he admitted.

Hannah remarked that she'd never had a great deal to do with digital forensics, so was very curious as to what it all entailed. 'Can a video just disappear like that after being played?' she asked.

Lex nodded. 'If it's set to work like that, then yes it can.'

Burton rocked back and forth in his seat, dipping so low that he temporarily vanished from view before reappearing again. 'Do you need to take the computer away?' he asked on one of his upright moments.

Lex declared that she did not as she would only need to do a parameter search, and in this case it meant searching for information coming into the computer from an outside source – but it was a little more complex than that. 'I'll be using my computer and forensic abilities to achieve a result,' she said.

'And how long could it take?' Burton asked when he was upright again.

'Well if the information has only just come in just now then it shouldn't take too long to track it down.' And with that Lex began to work her forensic magic, with Burton hopeful that it wouldn't take too long at all.

While Hannah watched Lex's dexterous fingers accessing the hidden recesses of the computer, Burton and Fielding grabbed a coffee and stood looking out of the window. The tinted windows hid the true nature of the weather, casting a greyness which would most likely be the same today in the month of November as it would be in the height of summer. They'd both finished their coffee when Lex asked them to come over.

Good, Burton thought, grateful that the whole procedure had taken less time than he'd imagined.

But then she delivered a bombshell it appeared even she hadn't expected. 'This is something I haven't come across before.' Her words hit them like a ton of bricks as she proceeded to elaborate on that sweeping statement. 'Usually – and by that I mean always – anything can be traced on a computer no matter how hard someone tries to hide it. In-depth system searches never fail. But this...' her voice trailed off as she wafted her hand towards the monitor, '...this is something beyond me, and I've been doing this for a good ten years now.'

'So what does that mean for us?' Although she fully realised the implications Fielding felt obliged to ask as Burton had the expression of a man defeated.

'Well the simple answer is, it's untraceable.' On hearing Burton's groan Lex continued with another option. 'But do you mind if I get one of my colleagues in here for their take on this?'

'By all means do,' he told her, chair once again dipping from sight to match his declining mood.

23

Whilst waiting for Lex to return with her colleague Burton decided to have a quick word with Hannah.

'Bearing in mind what was said on that video,' he began, 'I think that it might be wise for you to sit this one out for a while.'

Not one to mince words, Hannah told him right to his face what she thought about that ridiculous comment. 'You have got to be joking; I most certainly will not!' she declared, offended that he had even suggested it in the first place.

Although surprised by the response Burton continued regardless. 'But whoever this is has all but threatened your granddaughter.'

'Listen, Joe, I've been a police officer for more years than you've been alive and I can tell you that is never going to happen. I will tell my daughter to be vigilant, but she's always known what my job entails as I've never hidden any of that from her, so I'm sure that she will be in complete agreement with me on this.'

'Are you sure? Because this is now personal.'

'Yes, I am. It's been personal all along for me. William

Fielding was the best officer I've ever worked with, and he was my friend.' And with that the conversation ended. Hannah wasn't going to give an inch on this one. In the space of just a few days they had come across something so heinous that nothing and nobody was going to stop her from joining the search for the truth.

'But I do think we should tell Mrs Mendelson about this; tell her to be vigilant as well,' Fielding said. If the person on the video decided to put this plan into action then at least they had taken steps to try to prevent it by forewarning those implicated. Burton nodded. He'd go back and speak to the woman himself rather than just pick up the telephone and ring her. This just wasn't something that you tell someone over the phone.

There was a gentle rap on the door. It gave the impression that the person knocking had arrived in time to catch the end of the conversation. 'Is it okay to come in?' Lex asked, standing half in and half out of the partly-open door. From the shadow behind her it was apparent that she was not alone.

Fielding took over and invited her and her companion in as Hannah and Burton were still locking eyes with one another. She could see his point of view. In fact she could see both sides of the argument. Two young children had been potentially targeted, so of course he would be taking that stance. What had made it worse in his eyes was that one of the children was supposed to be Hannah's granddaughter, Millie. The figures in the video had been mannequins but, as the voice had said, the next time they could be the real deal.

Lex introduced her colleague, Matt Devonshire, and he raised a hand in greeting. Matt looked more in line with how they'd expected a digital forensic analyst to look like: a computer geek, with floppy hair and a pair of oversized horn-rimmed glasses hanging from his neck on an ethnic-design lanyard.

'I've explained everything to Matt and, luckily, I think he is the person to find this for you. But he's going to try something a little different to try to trace the origin of the video, if that's okay with you?'

'Yes, of course, try anything you feel would help.' Burton was grateful for anything at this point. They could take the whole thing apart and rebuild it again as far as he was concerned, as long as they managed to find out where the video had come from.

While Lex and Matt set to on the computer, Burton and the others stood by the window and watched and waited.

'Unusual name, Lex,' Fielding said. 'I'm assuming it's Alexis or Alexandra or the like?'

At which point Hannah thought it appropriate to impart her insider knowledge. 'No, I asked her about it before when we were sitting together; it's Lexus.'

'What, like the car?' Burton was astonished. 'Whoever names their children after cars?'

'Well, I've known a couple of people called Morris, spelled M-O-R-R-I-S, and they were both named after the car of the same name.'

Burton shook his head. 'Yes, but Morris – however you spell it – is still a regular name for a bloke. Whatever will parents think of next? Fiat, Skoda, Nissan?'

'I think that's taking it a bit too far!' Fielding laughed, but she could see where he was coming from. 'Besides,' she added, 'I quite like the name Lexus, and the shortened Lex; it sounds like a character from a science fiction book or film.'

Matt Devonshire appeared to be exactly the person for the job as it didn't take him long to find out what he was looking for. There were a few hurried words between himself and Lex, and a fair degree of pointing at the screen and then looking down at some sheets of paper he'd brought with him, before both turned to Burton and his team.

Matt explained, 'I knew about these but I've never actually been asked to try to trace one before.'

'Knew about what?' Burton hadn't a clue what the man was on about, nor did anyone else present who wasn't a tech wizard.

'They're self-destructing emails, designed to be viewed once then vanish completely from the mailbox. Some, like this particular one, are also designed to vanish entirely from the computer but, as you know, nothing is ever lost in cyberspace.'

'So how couldn't you find it, Lex?' Fielding asked, likewise amazed by Matt's speed in locating it and by his colleague's inability to do so.

'I've never seen one of these before. However, I knew that Matt had just attended a seminar in computer stealth and these types of emails were top of the agenda, especially as they seem to be becoming more and more popular. Isn't that right?'

Matt nodded frantically, seemingly ecstatic to have found one so soon after the lecture he'd been to. 'They're called confidentiality emails, designed not to be copied or shared, and the sender can decide how long it stays visible once it's sent to a recipient. Of course, whoever receives it can still take a screenshot, but often they won't have the time to do so as they won't realise that it will disappear shortly after viewed.'

'But you've found it?' Burton asked.

'Yes, I've found it,' Matt confirmed, indicating with a come-hither hand gesture that they should now all gather around the monitor. As they assembled, he pressed two keys simultaneously and the video reappeared in the centre of the screen and began to play. They all watched in silence while the one-minute recording ran its course before freezing on the last frame. 'There's only one thing, though,' Matt added when all eyes were still watching the haunting image. 'According to the tracking logs the video originated from this terminal.'

'Well yes,' Burton thought that he was stating the obvious, at least it was obvious to him if not to the others, 'that's where we viewed it. We all viewed it simultaneously on our own monitors.' But Matt was shaking his head.

'No, you misunderstand me,' he continued. 'What I mean is, the video originated from this terminal, and it appears that the time of origin was 23.51 yesterday evening.'

Now Burton understood. 'You mean,' he continued, 'that whoever sent us this video actually logged in to our system and sent it from here?'

'Exactly!' Matt proudly declared.

'So does the tracking log tell you who sent it and what their email address is?' Burton was becoming excited now. Finally, they would get to the bottom of who had sent this to them.

But when Devonshire told him, it certainly wasn't what he'd expected to hear. 'It's saying that you sent it, detective inspector.'

All eyes turned to Burton but all he could do was stare back in disbelief.

24

'But you know that that's not true!' Burton turned to Fielding. She of all people knew exactly where he was the previous evening when the threatening video had been sent: they had been sitting talking and discussing the case until midnight in the conservatory of her mother's house in Boldon.

'I know it's not,' she reassured him, knowing that he would want validation to be heard by the two tech people. 'Nobody is accusing you of anything; nobody ever would.'

Burton's hand instinctively went through his hair, one of his habits whenever he felt at a loss to understand something. 'But it's my login–'

It was Lex who cut in and stopped him this time. 'It's not your fault; anyone could have come into the building and done it.' Although he knew her words to be true it still wasn't acceptable for whoever it was to have used his credentials.

'Can we find out who?' Burton's eyes flicked from hers to her companion's, anxious for one of them to confirm that another person was responsible for it. He didn't like this ... he didn't like this one bit. Why implicate him, unless they were getting even closer to the person who was behind it all?

'We could look through the personnel logs for last night, but...' as Matt's voice trailed off everybody knew what was coming next, 'if they, whoever they are, are that good then I'm certain that they wouldn't let themselves be caught out by a security log, or a security camera come to that. It's evident to me that whoever has done this knows exactly how to cover their backs. A bit too much knowledge to my liking – professional, even. In fact, I'm pretty certain that they wanted the source of the video to be traced back to one of your terminals and your login details.'

Burton slumped down in his chair again. Fielding knew that this was torturing him. It was torturing all three of them. When this whole thing had begun, and when Hannah had told her that all was not as she and her family had been led to believe about her father's death all those years ago, all she wanted to do was to get to the truth about what had happened to him. She hadn't wanted to become embroiled in some cat-and-mouse game with a person or persons unknown who appeared to be able to manipulate the police IT systems.

Hannah herself must also be going through her own personal torture as well. She had seen what could have been her granddaughter in the video and she had already been threatened to stay away from the case. Fielding admired her for staying the course as, quite understandably, many others may not have reacted as she had done and taken themselves as far away from this as possible. Then there was Burton himself, brought into this of his own volition, but now so much in the thick of things that it was becoming difficult for him to know which way to turn.

'So we're stuck with this?' Burton asked nobody in particular and everyone in general.

'Yes.' Matt's statement was final and definitive.

At this point Fielding felt obliged to say her piece, as Burton's face was turning greyer by the second. 'We may well be stuck with this,' she told him, 'but we're waiting for other things to come back – like fingerprints from the box delivered to Hannah's daughter – and we need to get in touch with the chief constables in those other areas.' She hoped that this would bring him out of the depression he appeared to have sunk into.

'You're right!' he declared, leaping up out of his seat. 'Thank you both,' he said to Lex and Matt, 'you've been very helpful. If this person wants to play a game with us then I'm sure we can at least meet him or them halfway.'

That was more like the Burton she knew so well. Never one to give up or admit defeat. Criminals always slipped up ... always ... and this one was not going to get away from him or his team that easily.

After Lex and Matt had packed up their things and left, Burton decided to visit Doris Mendelson and give her the heads-up regarding her family's safety. He wasn't exactly certain what he would say to the woman when he got there, but that was something he could spend the hour's drive thinking about.

'Are you sure you don't want Hannah or myself to come along with you?' Fielding asked after he'd notified them of his intentions.

'No,' he said. 'You've got tasks to do here. Get on to those five forces about the signed-off investigations and DS Koder's cases.' Truth was, he also wanted time to think about what he had asked DCI Ambleton to try to find out for him.

'Okay, we can do that,' Fielding confirmed, eager to get started, and Hannah nodded in agreement. The video was horrible but Hannah was finding herself getting more and more immersed in this case. She realised that, perhaps, her joy at finally finding herself retired was not total. The events of the past few days seemed to support her realisation that her life as a police officer was not really over ... well, not for the time being at least, and now that she had started the ball rolling on the whole Jonas Burke question she wanted to see it through to the bitter end.

On his drive up to see Doris Mendelson, Joe Burton was so absorbed in the case that he hardly noticed the beauty of the Northumberland countryside. He was still waiting to hear from his boss about the request he had made to her, and that was bothering him just as much as the case he had now found himself working on.

He wasn't sure if he wanted the outcome of the request to go as he'd suspected, or whether he wanted it to be something he was way off the mark on. His hunches weren't usually wrong, but whichever way it turned out to be, he would still have to tell his partner about his suspicions.

Only a couple of curtains twitched this time when Burton drove into the cul-de-sac. It appeared that once a stranger had visited the village of Acomb and been welcomed into an inhabitant's house, they were no longer a stranger. *What is it about out-of-the-way communities?* Burton thought, harking back to the time Fielding had suggested that he watch the film, *The Wicker Man* – the Edward Woodward original version, not the Nicolas Cage remake, she'd insisted – where a police officer enters a community to solve a crime but things don't exactly go to plan. Burton always felt that he was being sized up for something a little similar himself.

He parked up outside Doris Mendelson's charming house, walked up the path and rang the doorbell. No response. Perhaps he should have called ahead. He was about to turn and leave, kicking himself for presuming that she would be at home, when he heard the chain being undone.

However, when he saw her standing there the relief of his journey not being for nothing turned into something else. She invited him in, and he followed her into the living room.

'What on earth happened?' he asked.

Doris had attempted to disguise it with make-up but she could not hide the fact that she was sporting one hell of a black eye.

'Oh that,' she tried to pass it off as nothing, 'I just tripped up over one of Jemima's toys yesterday.'

But Burton was not fooled. For one thing, he knew when someone was lying to him and he could tell by the tone of her voice that that this was indeed the case with her. 'Now come on–'

She held up a hand for him to stop. 'That's the truth, detective inspector; can we please leave it.' Before he had a chance to jump in and pursue it she added, 'Now why have you come to see me?'

Burton had gone over what he was going to say to her during the journey, but hadn't expected to see her in such a state as this. It momentarily distracted him from his purpose. 'I just wanted to make sure that you and your daughter were all right,' he told her.

'What do you mean?'

'Well… I…' he floundered. Not one usually stuck for words, all he could see when he looked at her was the black eye staring back at him. He didn't believe her story about falling over one of her daughter's toys, not for one minute. Come to think of it, where was her daughter?

'Is Jemima here with you?' he asked, looking around for evidence of her being there, discarded toys and the like, but the room looked tidy and devoid of any child's presence. Even the playpen was no longer in the corner.

'My mother has taken her for a few days,' Doris replied somewhat uneasily.

It was then that Burton decided to take a firmer stance with her. 'Look here, Mrs Mendelson,' his voice was perhaps firmer than intended, which only served to make the woman jump in shock, 'I want you to tell me exactly what has happened here!'

She moved towards the sofa to sit down, almost collapsing onto it as soon as she reached it, but still managed to maintain her composure regardless. However, Burton could see her eyes filling up with tears. 'I'd like you to leave now,' she demanded, but it was a half-hearted attempt to dismiss him.

He sat down beside her and rested a hand on hers. 'Please tell me what's wrong, Doris.' It was less of a demand this time and more of a compassionate question, but she shook her head defiantly.

'I can't,' she uttered. 'I just can't. I'd have far too much to lose. Now will you please go before–'

'Before what, Mrs Mendelson?'

'Before they know that you have been here!'

25

'She actually said that?' Fielding asked when he got back to headquarters. 'That she'd have too much to lose?'

He simply nodded his head in response. He'd wanted to push Doris Mendelson for further information, but could see that she was terrified of someone as she had actually told him that 'they' would know, meaning that there were multiple people involved.

'Do you think someone has threatened her daughter?' Fielding asked him. 'I'm bearing in mind the video we received.'

Burton shook his head. 'I just don't know what she meant, but she's certainly frightened by it and there have been physical threats made judging by the state of her eye. She can't tell me she got that from tripping over a toy.'

'And you didn't want to bring her in?' Hannah asked.

'No, but I think I need to check out what she told me, about her mother looking after the child. I need to know who her mother is and find out if that is true; I didn't want to push her any further for her name as she looked and sounded distraught, and I didn't like to mention the video either. Plus, there was the black eye. Secondly, what about the husband; where is he in all this? I want to know where he works and have a word with him as well. Is he also being threatened; or is he the person threatening his wife?'

'There is one thing that I've just realised,' Hannah spoke up. 'It's the name, Mendelson. It's German, isn't it?'

'Yes, I believe that it is,' Fielding confirmed. 'Like the composer, Mendelssohn.'

'Well, that's another German connection. It didn't register when the parcel arrived at my daughter's house, but now I think that it may well be relevant. What do you two think?'

Burton had to admit that two references to Germany couldn't just be coincidental, but what on earth did it mean? And what could the connection possibly be?

'What if it has something to do with Jonas Burke's real name?' Fielding offered.

'That's a very good point, and one we shall have to pursue as soon as his solicitor's court order comes through. He can't very well object once that is all done and dusted now can he?'

'This is outrageous,' said Fielding banging the phone down.

'Another no?' asked Burton, concern creasing his forehead. Not one person could help them in the five constabularies.

'Surely to goodness somebody worked on the cases!' said Fielding. 'Surely someone would have remembered being there when it happened and filing a report.'

Apparently not, according to the responses they got. Had the officers been told to say that when anyone questioned them about it? It was certainly beginning to look that way.

Burton was frustrated, and so was Fielding. This response was completely unacceptable to both of them. What on earth could they do to find this information out?

Hannah came back from the coffee machine with two mugs which she set down for Fielding and Burton. 'Perhaps I'll have better luck finding the two officers in charge of that boy in the pantry case,' she said soothingly as she returned to her desk.

They had a better time locating Doris Mendelson's mother and husband. What had initially seemed like a difficult task turned out to be quite an easy one. Hannah had suggested trying the local nursery school in Acomb in the hope that Jemima Mendelson might be attending there some days a week. She remembered that her own granddaughter had obtained a pre-nursery place when she was aged two and thought that just maybe Doris had managed to do the same thing.

The school's head teacher was initially cautious, and quite rightly so. 'I'll hang up and call you back at the police headquarters if you don't mind,' she said. A few minutes later the control room transferred her back to Burton's phone, and she gave them the information they required. Burton also checked that Jemima was in school at that moment, which she was.

Doris Mendelson's mother, Claudia Simpson, was shocked when she answered the telephone. 'Is everything all right with Doris?' she asked with an urgency Fielding found a little disturbing. Was she aware of what was really going on?

'Yes,' Fielding told her, 'nothing to worry about, this is just a courtesy call. Are you concerned that anything might not be?'

'What do you mean?'

'I'm referring to her black eye. Has she told you how she got that?'

'Why yes, she tripped over one of Jemima's toys. Actually, I'm a little concerned about her balance of late, and suggested that she see her doctor about it.'

'What do you mean her balance?' Fielding tried to get more information out of her. 'Has she had falls like this before then?'

'A couple of days ago she had some bruises on her arms,' said she walked into the door frame of all things. You can see why I'm so concerned about her.' Mrs Simpson seemed genuinely worried about her daughter's health.

Fielding continued with the questioning. 'So why do you have your granddaughter at the moment?'

'Doris said that she was going to go to see her GP, and I suggested that I have Jemima stay over here for a couple of days to give her time to try and get the condition sorted out. I remember how hard it is bringing up a two-year-old, more so if she's having dizzy spells, and she seemed happy for me to spend the time with Jemima. It would give her a break, she said, and I was more than happy to help in any way that I could.'

At the end of the conversation Fielding thanked Mrs Simpson for her time. However, she was not entirely happy that Doris Mendelson was simply having dizzy spells, as her mother had described them.

Burton had located Doris's husband, Frank not too far from police headquarters, and decided to pay him a visit and speak to the man face-to-face. He worked in a large bank's offices at the Cobalt Centre and he was more than happy to speak to the detective, although not quite sure why he wanted to discuss anything with him in the first place. Frank Mendelson was one of the IT department team leaders there, and after their initial meeting he took the detective up to his floor and into one of the side offices. Burton felt a bit conspicuous sitting there as the room was transparent, constructed completely of floor to ceiling glass panels. What made it even more uncomfortable was that the members of staff sitting at their desks kept turning around to look at him, so it seemed that one pair of eyes or another was always looking his way. He felt as if he was at an interview, and being judged and scored by each member of staff independently.

'Tell me, Mr Mendelson,' he began, trying to overcome the

curiosity of those around him, 'your wife's black eye ... how exactly did she get it?'

Mendelson appeared to be confused. 'I'm assuming that you've spoken to her, so I don't doubt that she's told you all about that.' And then the penny dropped. 'Now hang on! You can't think that I did that to her, can you?'

Burton had to admit that he wasn't certain, but he simply said, 'Of course not.'

But Mendelson wasn't having any of that. 'Has one of my neighbours said something to the police?'

'Why would any of them say that then, sir?'

Mendelson looked Burton straight in the eye. 'It's that damned writer, isn't it?' he said venomously. 'I'm sure a lot of them are jealous of her collection of memorabilia on him.'

Burton could hardly believe that to be possible, but his experience in this area was limited. Burke had a huge fan following; and if one person decided to start a collection of his works and all the associated paraphernalia, and had actually met the man on more than one occasion, then perhaps jealousy from another one of his admirers could boil over into something more sinister?

'Has one of them accused me of giving her that black eye?' Mendelson continued with no less anger than a few moments ago.

'No one is accusing you of anything, sir,' Burton reassured the IT manager, which seemed to calm him down again.

'Then why are you here?'

That's not an easy question, thought Burton. He had thought that, with their current investigation, Mrs Mendelson may have said something to them that she wasn't supposed to and Burke had sent someone around to silence her. But that premise relied upon Burke being somehow involved in all of this and the police corruption, and at this stage he had no firm evidence upon which to base that assumption. So it was all conjecture and he had to reply carefully to this question. He simply said, 'Something's come up regarding Jonas Burke's research and we're trying to get to the bottom of it.'

'Like what?' Frank Mendelson pushed Burton, perhaps thinking that he was entitled to an answer since the detective had come to his place of work and all but accused him of giving his wife a shiner.

'Well I can't really say at the moment.'

'And you think, what, that my wife got a black eye because of this?'

Burton could tell that Mendelson wasn't going to let this go. He probably wouldn't either if he was in the same position. He shook his head and just told Mendelson that he really didn't know what to think at this point. 'If you do see anything that looks out of the ordinary, any strange cars driving into your cul-de-sac, or any strangers hanging around, I'd appreciate it if you could give me a call.'

'Sure,' Mendelson told him, 'but do I say anything to my wife?'

'Best not to at the moment. It could simply be as she says and she fell over one of your daughter's toys–'

'What do you mean fell over one of Jemima's toys?' Mendelson appeared startled by the statement and continued. 'She told me that she tripped on the corner of the rug and fell against the edge of the table.'

'Maybe that's exactly what she did after tripping over your daughter's toy and didn't want to blame her for it?' Burton put to him, but he had already suspected that Mrs Mendelson might be trying to cover up the truth of what had really happened.

Casting a hasty glance sideways, he found himself still being observed by the employees. 'Right then,' he announced, preparing to make his move, 'like I said, just keep a watch out for anything that looks out of the ordinary.'

'The village is small, well you've seen it, haven't you, so anything out of the ordinary would be noticed by someone. We're a tight-knit community who stick together, and any sign of an intruder would have alarm bells going off, and I don't mean figuratively.' Mendelson rose from his chair sensing that Burton was bringing the interview to a close, but before leaving the detective asked one final question.

'Your name,' he began, 'it's German, isn't it?'

'Polish-German actually,' Frank Mendelson told him. 'My paternal grandfather was in Germany during the war years, but got out as soon as he could and came to live in England. Never went back there. Can't say that I'd want to either given the circumstances. Why do you ask?'

'Just something that came up; not really important, but I thought that I would ask.' And with that the two men shook hands and Mendelson led Burton from the glass box. He could feel the eyes on his back as he was led through the office and along to the lift.

'Any luck?' Fielding asked when Burton arrived back at the office from interviewing Frank Mendelson, husband of super-fan Doris Mendelson.

'No, the man seems clean to me. I don't think he has anything to do with either this or his wife's black eye. However, it's the business with his name that I'm now concerned with.'

Hannah was very quiet, concentrating heavily on the job in hand.

'Like you thought, Hannah, he is German,' he told her and she looked up at the sound of her name. 'Well, German-Polish,' he continued, 'and there's another connection I'm concerned about.'

It was Fielding who spoke up at this point. 'There are far too many coincidences here,' she observed.

Burton nodded. 'Far too many for my liking.' He didn't like loose ends and things that were 'off kilter', as he always put it, and this whole case seemed to have far too many of both for him. 'I think I'll check on Angela Fairbanks's house this evening; see if anybody pulls up in a white van or parks nearby.'

'You could be there all night,' Fielding told him, and he shook his head.

'No, I'm not planning on an all-nighter, just a couple of hours around, say, eight to ten o'clock, and if nobody shows up by then I'll call it quits.'

'Well if you're sure.'

'Yes, I think that loose end needs to be pursued as well.'

Mrs Fielding made sure that Joe Burton left the house that evening before going out on his 'stake-out' with a full stomach.

'Mum, you've been watching far too many crime shows,' Sally laughed at her description of what her partner intended to do that evening.

'Isn't that what they're called?' her mother asked in all seriousness. 'I'm sure I've heard it called that before.'

'Most likely on American TV shows,' Burton told her, 'but it does creep into our vocabulary now and again. We just tend to call it surveillance over here, that's all.'

'He's not going to be out all night, you know,' Sally said.

'No, but he's going to be gone for two hours, just sitting in a car. He needs feeding up.'

Sally laughed out loud. The thought of Joe Burton needing 'feeding up' tickled her more than her mother understood. The man could sit down and eat anything at any time of the day, and certainly didn't go without where food was concerned. She looked at him and he just smiled, knowing what would be going through her mind. All he could do was shrug his shoulders and say, 'If your mother feels the need to feed me up, then who am I to refuse!'

Mrs Fielding had to admit that she was enjoying the banter between these two ever since Joe had arrived in Boldon. A bit like Hannah Sanderson, she too could see something more in their relationship than just a working partnership. It was the way that they looked at one another, the casual way in which they poked fun at one another and, perhaps more importantly, they both were completely dependent upon the other. It stood out to her but, like Hannah, she wasn't entirely sure if they knew what their true feelings for one another were.

'Right,' Joe said, finishing the last mouthful of pie, 'that's me done,' indicating that he was all set to go on his 'stake-out', as Mrs Fielding had so quaintly put it.

'Are you sure you don't want to take a flask of coffee with you?' Mrs Fielding asked.

'Mum!' Sally declared. The feast he had just eaten had been quite enough for two hours in a car keeping watch on a house.

'Well he might get thirsty,' her mother told her, referring to her house guest in the third person even though he was standing right beside her.

'I'll be fine, Mrs Fielding,' he told her. 'Now don't you be worrying about me, I'm a big boy you know!'

'Just wrap up warm then,' she added as he was closing the front door behind him, and his hand went up in the air to give her a wave. Although grateful for the offer of a flask, he had thoughts of another way to get his caffeine fix.

Right then, he thought. *I'm sure I saw a Costa right next to that shopping outlet.*

27

As he sat in the car with his coffee cup in the drinks holder, Joe Burton settled down to watch Angela Fairbanks's house from across the street. He'd found what he'd thought to be the ideal spot to watch it from without being too noticeable, and had backed the car up into a small turning so that he could get a clear view of whatever may or may not happen in the next couple of hours. He'd found the house again and the Costa he thought he'd caught sight of on his first visit there.

So with latte close by he sat and waited. He was not really expecting to see anything, but had decided to play it safe just in case. Tying up loose ends again.

There are not many ways to amuse yourself whilst out in a car on surveillance. One way is to try and keep yourself warm. He had wrapped up warm, as Mrs Fielding had suggested, but it was still chilly in the car with the heater off. He did turn it on now and again just to get the circulation going through to his fingers again.

Thankfully it was getting close to his deadline of ten o'clock. About ten minutes to go and then he could head back to Boldon.

He wasn't happy that this had all been for nothing, but just at that moment he saw movement from across the road. A white van came to a stop a few houses down from Angela's, and its headlights were turned off. Instinctively, he hit the camera button on his phone and took a shot of the number plate. If this was the same van as the one in the CCTV then her plates would have been ditched as soon as their usefulness was over.

He watched as a man in a hoodie got out of the passenger side, holding something which Burton couldn't initially make out as it appeared to be covered in a cloth of some kind. Then part of the cloth fell loose and he could see a number plate beneath it.

This is it! he thought, and began snapping away again. He tried to get a shot of the driver, but whoever it was behind the wheel was sitting in darkness. He took the shot nevertheless, in the knowledge that someone back at headquarters could possibly clean it up to get a much sharper image.

The man who had got out of the passenger side walked up to Angela Fairbanks's house and up her front drive. A wheelie bin was standing in front of a gate, which Burton presumed led to the back garden, and, lifting the lid, the man dropped the number plate inside before turning and hurrying back to the van. It was quite a bold move considering the living room light was on, albeit the curtains were drawn. Once back in the vehicle, it slowly moved away with the headlights left off.

Burton could hardly believe his luck – or the man's brazenness. The number plates had been covered in a cloth, but suspected that they must have been touched at some point, so realised that he had to go and retrieve them from the bin. But that in itself was a puzzling thing. Surely the plates could have been dumped anywhere, so why put them into Angela Fairbanks's bin? Had they been told to do that by whoever hired them? That seemed the only feasible reason he could think of.

Dumping them randomly might arouse suspicion, but how many people these days saw discarded number plates and handed them into the police? None, if any. There had to be a reason, but what it was eluded him.

He decided not to worry Angela Fairbanks at this time. He didn't wish to distress the woman any more. Clearly, she wasn't in any way connected to whoever it was who had used her plates but, there again, depositing her plates at her address gave rise to an even bigger question. How on earth did they know where she lived? To retrieve somebody's address through their number plates you had to have professional access to the DVLA database. You'd have to be in touch with somebody who worked there, or, somebody in the police force. Alarm bells sounded in Burton's head, and they seemed to ring out the name 'Paul Winters'.

He was now in two minds what to do: Should he trail the van? But now he had what assumed were its true number plates he could trace the owner through the databases back at the office. He quickly checked his phone to make sure he had good, clear shots of its registration details, and he had. What he did want to do, though, was to make note of what he'd just witnessed in his notebook. He reached inside the left side of his jacket pocket, but it wasn't there. He tried the other pocket just in case he'd slipped it in there by mistake, but no, it wasn't there either. It was then that he visualised it beside the phone on his desk just before leaving for the evening, and he couldn't recall having picked it up.

In a split second, as he didn't have his book, he decided to follow the van. If the bin was out for the next day's collection then he could come back later and retrieve the number plates after he'd found out where the van finally parked up. He could go back to the office after that, as he knew it stayed open twenty-four hours a day monitored by a security officer on reception, and double-check the address in the database and also find out who the van's registered keeper was.

He watched the van drive off down the street then turned the ignition on and followed it, keeping a fair distance back. As there wasn't that much traffic on the road, he would stand out if he got too close.

He had no idea where he was, let alone know where he was going, but he made sure that he kept the white van within his sights. One distraction, one missed turning, and it would have all been for nothing. After about fifteen minutes it pulled onto a driveway, came to a stop and so did he, some way back, turning his lights off. The only thing he did know was that he was still on the north side of the river as he hadn't had to go through the tunnel. Chatting and laughing, the two men got out and went into the house. Burton took out his phone to see where he was located and took a screenshot; that at least gave him the address, and the camera on his phone provided him with the number. Satisfied, he reprogrammed his maps to take him back to Angela Fairbanks's house to pick up the plates.

As luck would have it there was now a car on the driveway and the bin was nowhere to be seen.

'Dammit!' Burton said out loud, knowing that he was now going to have to knock on the door. Unless ... yes, he'd try that. He parked in the spot he'd found earlier and quickly made his way up the drive and tried the gate. It was open.

Keeping as quiet as he could he opened the bin lid and found the plates still right at the top. At least they hadn't dropped down to the bottom when it had been moved. Picking them out he gently closed the lid and went back through the gate, then back to his car. He could see that the light was still on in the living room, but there was no movement from within. Thankfully, nobody had seen or heard him.

28

After a hurried call to Sally to say what he'd been doing he drove the relatively short distance back to police headquarters. The security officer on reception greeted him as he entered.

'You're having a late one,' the man said, rising from his chair and putting the after-hours ledger on top of the desk.

'Yes, just wanting to check up on something,' Burton said, picking up a pen and signing himself in. He glanced at the clock above the officer's head – 10.45 – and jotted the time down alongside his name.

'You're not the only one, it seems,' the man behind the desk said, and Burton looked at him curiously.

'Oh?' he asked, wondering who else could be in at this time of night.

'A couple of members of the tech crew came in about twenty minutes ago. Said they needed to work on something important before the morning. So if you hear noises then it's most likely them. They're up on the second floor.'

'Same as me. Okay then,' Burton said, 'if I hear something

then I'll know that it's them. I'm not staying long, maybe fifteen minutes or so.'

'Well I'll still be here when you come down,' the man laughed. 'I'm here until eight in the morning!'

Burton smiled through gritted teeth. 'You have my sympathy.'

'Oh I'm used to it by now.' The officer could make light of his schedule, as the nightshift had been his routine now for the past few weeks.

Friendly chat over, Burton made his way over to the lift and pressed the call button. It must have been on the ground floor as it opened almost immediately for him and he stepped into it. When the lift stopped at the second floor the doors opened to an eerie sight. The entire floor was in darkness, and it wasn't until he put one foot into the corridor that a light flickered on above him. As he kept moving forward more lights sprung into life and he realised that they were presence detector lights, automatically coming on at night when someone walks past them. They didn't have them in Manchester. *Good idea*, he thought.

He heard the voices long before he saw them, and they seemed to be in an office close to his. As he reached the point in the corridor where he needed to turn left, he rounded the corner but then stopped suddenly and took a few hasty steps backwards. Not only were the people the voices belonged to near to his office, they were actually in it. He couldn't quite make out what was being said, but there seemed to be an awful lot of activity going on in there with constant talking and the sound of someone rummaging around.

Backed up against the wall he took out his phone and found the voice recorder app and switched it on. He had to somehow get closer to pick up what they were saying, so he dropped down to the ground and crawled around commando-style until he thought he was close enough to use it successfully.

He didn't even think for one moment what he would do if they decided to pack up and go as he wouldn't be able to get up from the floor and back to the safety of hiding around the corner again in such a short space of time. But he had to know what they were saying, and record it as evidence.

'I really don't like this,' a female voice said.

A male one answered her. 'We've got our instructions.'

'I know but–'

The man interrupted her. 'You know what'll happen if we don't do as we're told.'

'I know, but,' the woman again, 'it doesn't mean that I've got to like it.'

'I didn't like it either when I had to give that woman a black eye, but we have our instructions.'

So that's how Doris Mendelson got her black eye, Burton thought. He didn't recognise the voices. At first he thought that it might be Lex and her colleague Matt, but it definitely wasn't either of them. What exactly had they been told to do, and what would happen if they didn't do it? The two questions puzzled Burton but of one thing he was sure, this had to be related to what they were investigating.

'Okay, I think that's enough,' the man finally said, and Burton took that as his cue to retreat to somewhere out of view. Moving as quietly as he could, he managed to crawl back to the corner then get up. The next problem of course was, which direction were they going to leave the building in? If they decided to come his way then he'd definitely be spotted, so what to do? Looking around quickly he saw an opportunity not only to hide but also to get a closer look at who the two people were. The door to the office across the corridor was slightly ajar, so if he could get himself into there and hide in the darkness then he might just manage to take a photo of them coming out of his office. But then there was the overhead lighting to think of. The one where he was hiding had just gone off, but if he started to move it would most certainly come on again. And then, what about the lights in the office, would they come on too? He had no other option; it was a chance he was going to have to take.

As expected, the corridor light picked up his movement and he ran across to the door. Fortunately, the lights inside the office stayed off; he'd escaped that at least. As he crouched down below the glass panel he willed the corridor light to dim itself once again, which it did just seconds before the man and the woman exited his office. He'd already managed to make sure that the flash on his phone was turned off, so he took a quick camera roll shot of them in the doorway before ducking down out of sight again. Fortunately, they turned right after coming out of the office and headed off to the flight of stairs just beyond.

Burton breathed a sigh of relief. He could feel the sweat trickling down his face.

After waiting for what he considered an acceptable length of time to make sure they didn't return, Burton went to see what had been going on in the room. He turned the light switch on and looked around; everything seemed very much as it had done when he, Sally and Hannah had left for the evening. So what had they been doing? Hadn't the officer on duty downstairs told him that they had signed themselves in as tech, so if that was the case then they must have been going through their computers. But for what? Just to see what information they had gathered over the course of the past few days? As he wasn't all that tech-minded he wouldn't know what to look for that was amiss should he try to find out. But what he could do was take photos of the room as it now stood, and around their workstations. Maybe one of the others might see something non-cyber out of place.

He found his notebook not quite where he thought that he'd left it, lying on top of his keyboard. He would never have put it there! He quickly made notes about what he'd seen outside Angela Fairbanks's house and what had happened thereafter.

Then he turned on his computer and began the search for the owner of the white van.

What he found surprised him, but the address was not as expected... However, that was something that he'd have to check out in the morning. He was just about to call it a night when he heard a noise behind him. He turned to look around, but the last thing he saw was a fist heading straight for his face.

29

When he came around he was lying flat out on the floor with a pain in his head equal to that in his nose. He put a hand instinctively up to his face; the area around his nostrils felt wet and sticky and extremely tender to the touch. His fingers were the colour of strawberry jam. He raised his head and looked around him, trying to find something to wipe his face with. It was then that he noticed his phone lying on the floor nearby; its screen was smashed. He picked it up and tried the power switch, but nothing was working. All the photos he'd taken at Angela Fairbanks's house of the man who'd got out of the white van and the driver were on there. All he could find to wipe his nose on was the back of his hand.

'What on earth happened to you?' the security guard asked, quickly handing him an open box of facial tissues when he managed to get himself downstairs. 'Do you need me to call a medic for you?'

Burton refused his offer, taking a tissue and wiping it across his face. As one wasn't enough he took a handful.

'The two tech people who came in earlier, did you manage to get their names by any chance?'

'Why yes,' he told him, pointing to the ledger on the desk.

Burton went over to take a look, but what he saw didn't make any sort of sense at all.

'What about CCTV?' he asked, pointing up to the camera behind the guard.

'Yes, that's on all the time.'

'Will I be able to get a copy of it in the morning?'

'I'll make sure that you will.'

To say Sally Fielding was shocked when she saw her partner's face was something of an understatement. Apart from the pain in both his head and nose, he was now having a problem with his vision, and had struggled to drive himself back to the house in Boldon.

'My goodness, Joe, what happened?' she spluttered, looking him over and thinking that perhaps she should take him down to A&E.

'Just let me sit down and I'll tell you.'

Fielding led him into the living room where he all but fell onto the sofa.

Mrs Fielding, having heard the commotion, had come downstairs from her bedroom to see what was going on. On seeing his appearance she immediately went into the kitchen and returned with a bowl, a facecloth and a towel.

Sally took them from her mother and sat beside him with the bowl on her knees and proceeded to wipe his face with the damp facecloth.

'Ouch!' He winced when it touched his nose, but she worked quickly and soon had his face cleaned up. The only thing was, his nose appeared to be twice the size it had been before he'd gone out for the evening.

'I think you should get this checked out at the hospital,' she told him.

'We've only got until Friday to get this case sorted out–'

'But we can continue working on it from Manchester if we have to,' she insisted, 'and I think this needs to get checked.'

Burton looked towards Mrs Fielding for support, but she only told him that she agreed with her daughter.

'Okay, okay,' he gave in. 'As long as you drive.'

'Well I wasn't going to let you drive in that state,' she chided him, while her mother stood nodding in the background.

Once in the car he told her what had happened.

'And you didn't see who it was?'

'No, it was just a blur and then blackness. But, get this, the security guard checked the signing-in book and the supposed names of the two tech people were Burke and Mendelson.

'That can't be their real names though; they must have used false identities to log in.'

'The guard would also have checked their photo IDs, like he did mine,' he told her, but Fielding wasn't convinced by this.

'Anyone can forge an identity photo, and the name on it come to that. I mean ... come on ... Mendelson and Burke ... that's just too ridiculous to even consider them to be their real names. They've just used them to fool us.'

'I suppose you're right. Fortunately they will have been caught on CCTV, and the guard said that we could get the footage in the morning. I did have shots of the two people in the white van at Angela Fairbanks's house, but I can't get my phone to turn on now. It looks like it's been stamped on or something.'

'We can do a facial recognition in the morning,' Sally suggested, 'and perhaps get Lex or Matt to look at your phone.'

'Yes, I think that's a good idea.'

'So did you manage to check for the van's owner before you were knocked out,' she asked after a pause, and was again shocked by the answer he gave her.

'The guy's in banking, so what on earth could Doris Mendelson's husband want with a van?'

'What do you mean a white van?' Mendelson had exploded when Burton rang him up the next morning. 'I don't own a bloody white van. Who on earth has told you that, who's feeding you this information? This is bordering on harassment, Burton!'

Burton tried to keep it together. His nose was still hurting, though the hospital had confirmed that it hadn't been broken, and he wasn't prepared to stand for any nonsense from anyone today. 'The DVLA has fed me this information, sir. You're on record as being the registered owner.'

'Well I'm not!' Mendelson was almost shouting at him down the phone and Burton had to hold the receiver at arm's length away from his ear. As Sally and Hannah looked across at him the line went dead.

'Great,' Burton said, replacing the phone on the receiver.

'What if,' Hannah began, 'the DVLA records have also been doctored? Mr Mendelson sounded genuinely shocked by that news.'

Burton groaned and put his head on the desk. 'This case is getting more complicated by the minute,' he said with a muffled voice before lifting his head again. 'I feel it's become much more than looking into your father's death, Sally.'

'I know what you mean,' she agreed with him. 'It's definitely gone way beyond that now.'

'In all seriousness, unless Burke's advisor is a skilled computer wizard I think that we're also looking for a hacker who is gaining access into our systems and, by the look of it, the DVLA's ones.'

'Shouldn't we be getting lab results back today for the fingerprints?' Hannah asked. 'Both from the box and from Burke's book?'

'And the court order for Burke's solicitor,' Fielding joined in.

'Let's hope so,' Burton said, 'and let's hope something turns up from both.'

He had taken his phone along to Lex and Matt, who had promised to try their best. But, of course, things are never that easy. By late morning the results from the lab were sent to Burton's email address, but they were not the results that he'd hoped for.

'No, no, no!' Burton declared upon reading it, banging both fists down on the desk. 'No fingerprints on the box with the pig's snout other than those of your daughter, Hannah. And a multitude on the book, but none matching anything we have on record.'

It was such a blow, as prints on the pig snout box could have confirmed who the van driver was. And those on the book might have confirmed Burke's true identity.

With regards to the van, Fielding had suggested that the DVLA database might also have been tampered with, and he began to think that it could indeed be the case. Mendelson may well be as innocent as he claimed and simply just another pawn in somebody's game designed to throw them off the truth. *It must be one hell of a truth*, he thought.

'I might have something for us,' Hannah told them, pressing a button and the printer sprung into action. 'I've tracked down former DI Martin Scott and DS Barry Small, those two less-than-charming officers in charge of the boy in the pantry case.'

'Good, good!' Burton seemed relieved to at last get some sort of a concrete lead. 'Where are they located; do they still live locally?'

'As suspected they are both retired, and one lives at The Nook in South Shields and the other in Gateshead.'

'I don't know where that is,' Burton admitted. 'Are they both local?'

When Hannah told him that they were, he asked her, 'Are you up to paying them a visit, or would you prefer not to see them again?'

They were the last two people she had ever wanted to see after DI Martin Scott's humiliation of her. She had never borne a grudge in her life, but he still appeared to be bothering her after all these years. Yet at the same time she was curious about the people they had ended up as, so told Burton that she would go along with him.

'I'll give them a call and let them know we're visiting. Sally, if you could stay by the inbox and check for when the court order comes through, then perhaps we could get that all-important call through to Burke's solicitor before he leaves for the night.'

'Will do,' she confirmed.

Their first stopping off point was Gateshead, to see former DS Barry Small. Hannah hadn't intended to mention that they had met once all those years ago as there was no need for her to do so. *In any case*, she thought, *he wouldn't remember me in the slightest from when I was a newly qualified female constable.*

Burton was desperate to know how the report on the case had been filed and by whom.

Barry Small was not how Burton had pictured him. Perhaps it was his name that instantly gave the impression of him being someone of limited stature, but that couldn't have been further from the truth. The man mountain towered above Burton's six-foot frame, making him at least six four, six five perhaps, and for a man of his age he had an almost enviable flurry of thick, white hair.

'Come in, come in,' he said, giving Burton's nose a quick glance as he ushered him and Hannah into his home.

'It was a very long time ago,' the man said after taking a look at the file Burton had handed him, 'and my memory is not as good as it used to be, son.'

Burton's heart sank once again. One concrete lead and it looked as if it was going to end up as a dead end.

'Marty might remember a bit better than me; he's still on the ball after all these years. But reading all this again, I have to say that it is a bit familiar. It was an unusual case as I recall though.'

'Unusual?' Burton quizzed him. 'Why is that then?'

'Can't quite remember all of it, but it was one that stuck in my mind for a very long time after that. Before my memory started to fade, that is.'

Even though the man said that he couldn't recall, Burton tried to jog his memory a bit. 'So did your DI fill in the report, can you recall?'

'He would have done; he used to do all that himself. Sometimes he'd ask me, but not very often.'

'Do you recall a DS Koder at the time?'

Burton could see the man searching for the name, and he didn't feel hopeful for recognition.

'I can't say I do. But like I say—'

'Yes, I understand.' Burton had no intention of pushing Small any further than necessary, as his memory problems seemed to be a big issue with him. 'Okay, we'll leave it there, Mr Small. Thank you for your time and for seeing us.'

'Can I ask, why did you ask about the name Koder?' A sudden spark of interest spurred Burton on again.

'His name was on the file as being the senior investigating officer and he signed the case off as unsolved—'

'Well that can't be right,' Small insisted. 'Marty always filled in the reports, I know that for a fact. And there was only me and him investigating it, just like each case we were on.'

'That's what we feared,' Burton said more to himself than Small.

30

A fter leaving Barry Small's house they hoped that his former DI might be of more assistance, so Burton changed the address locator to his.

'Nice house for someone on a police salary,' commented Hannah as they pulled up outside Martin Scott's impressive double-fronted mansion in South Shields.

Meaning what? Burton thought. *Is she implying that Scott had obtained money from a non-work source to pay for it?* 'Perhaps his wife has a good job too,' Burton suggested, not wishing to jump to untimely conclusions, although, he had to admit, he wouldn't be able to afford something as luxurious as this either – unless he had a big win on the lottery. The well-known gardener, Alan Titchmarsh, would have been proud of the well-stocked front garden, and the perfect topiary box trees looked as if they were regularly and professionally maintained.

They came to a stop on the road just past the gates. A BMW was parked up on the neat gravel driveway, new by the look of the registration plates, and Burton took a quick look inside the driver's side before continuing up to the front door. The interior was immaculate, with a fresh-out-of-the-showroom look, so it appeared to be a very recent purchase.

Hannah pressed the doorbell beside the imposing front door while Burton was still looking the car over. He hurried to her side as the door opened. Although not as tall as his former DS, Martin Scott was still a tall man, six one Burton judged him to be. Upon introducing themselves, Hannah noticeably flinched as he looked the two of them over before reaching out and taking Burton's outstretched hand. He didn't take Hannah's, but only gave her a look of what could quite easily pass as disdain, and it brought that whole incident of her youth back to her. *Horrible, horrible man!* she thought. *Time hasn't changed his view of women, it seems. Misogynistic bastard!*

Burton felt very uncomfortable by the way Scott chose to ignore Hannah, and as they followed Scott into the house he mouthed, 'Are you okay?' to her and she nodded.

Martin Scott plonked himself down on an armchair. 'Please sit down,' he told them, indicating the sofa across the room. It only reinforced Burton's dislike of him; the man had no manners whatsoever.

'So you've spoken to Brian?' he asked. His eyes were on Burton, not even a flicker in Hannah's direction.

'Yes we have just been to see him and, sadly, he says that his memory is not what it used to be, so he couldn't really help us with what we wanted to ask him.'

Scott smirked. 'Yes, Brian's gone a bit gaga over the years.'

Burton was disgusted, and corrected his rather crude assessment of his former partner. 'You mean he has a touch of Alzheimer's?'

'If you mean that he's lost his marbles, then yes.'

Burton could sense Hannah seething beside him simply by the change in her breathing pattern. Her breaths were long and deep, as if she was trying to control what she was feeling. He could fully understand what she was going through. The man was a pig.

'So, Mr Scott,' Burton continued, handing over the manila envelope which contained the file, 'if you'd like to take a look at this and tell me what you think.'

Martin Scott opened the envelope and took its contents out. He quickly skimmed it then put it down on his lap. 'I don't understand,' he said. 'What am I looking at? This case is decades old!'

'I know it is,' Burton said keeping his cool. The man still hadn't acknowledged the woman sitting next to him, and that made his blood boil, 'but take a look at the signature at the bottom; isn't that where you would have signed off the case yourself, being the SIO?'

Scott reopened the file, and Burton could see his eyes resting on the bottom of the page. His eyebrows creased momentarily before looking up again.

'I don't know who this is,' he motioned to the signature. 'It's not mine. I know for a fact that I signed this case off. Who the hell's this Koder person?'

'That's what we would like to know,' Burton told him, adding, 'How do you remember the case so well if I may ask? You said that it was decades old?'

'I could never forget that one,' he said. 'It was the first one that Brian and I worked on as a team in 1983. You never forget your first, isn't that what they say? Anyway, it was one of the most unusual cases I've ever had to deal with.'

'Why's that then?' Hannah offered her first words of the meeting, which took Scott completely off guard. He looked at her with a look that quite visibly said 'how dare you speak to me', but she continued now that she had started. 'Why that one in particular, Mr Scott?'

Her stress on the word 'Mr' impressed Burton. Hannah

appeared to be rubbing in the fact that he was no longer that bigshot DI who bullied young female constables, and she could now speak to him in any way she felt fit.

Scott had no choice but to answer her and to look at her as he did. 'There was something very off with the crime scene and it just didn't sit right with either me or Brian,' he remembered.

'In what way?' Burton asked. He'd had a few cases himself in the past that didn't feel quite right to him and was curious to know why this former DI had felt that way.

'Well for one thing, everything was too neat, too precise. The windowpane in the back door had been broken, which is how the assailant must have got in, but...' He paused for a moment before directing the next question at Burton and again ignoring Hannah. 'You know when you get that feeling that all is not as it seems? Well that's just how it felt to me. For one thing, we found a lot of glass on the outside path which suggested to me it was broken from the inside, but then again there was the boy to consider.'

'The boy?' Hannah asked. 'You mean that poor, scared boy in the pantry?'

'Yes ... that's the one. How–' He looked at her curiously, wondering how she could possibly know that. The boy was mentioned in the report, but from what she was saying it sounded as if she'd actually been there.

'You don't recognise me, do you, Scott?' Hannah asked him before he could ruminate on that any further. Burton was enjoying this.

He looked at her long and hard. 'No, should I?'

'Well it has been decades,' she echoed his words about the age of the case, 'and I was only a humble lady constable.'

Recognition finally set in. 'You were that female who contaminated the scene by throwing up?'

'Yes. It's a shame that I didn't throw up all over you.' Hannah finally let go of all the years of holding the memory of that horrible day in.

'Now listen here–' Scott began, but Burton jumped in.

'So can you remember the boy's name? There's no mention of it in the file.'

Scott scowled at Hannah before picking up the file and reading it again, 'Well there was when I filed it; there seems to have been some things changed in here. Even though I said that it was a case I couldn't forget, the one thing I don't remember is that boy's name. I'd try some nuthouse or another if I were you.'

'Now why on earth would you say that, Mr Scott?'

'The boy looked disturbed.'

'Well he would do, wouldn't he?' Hannah intervened. 'He'd most likely witnessed his father being murdered.'

'No, there was something else I felt, something about him that was off.'

After that all three fell silent before Burton broke the silence. 'One last question, Mr Scott.' Burton was determined to deliver this one last after he'd gleaned as much information out of the man as possible as he fully expected to be thrown out of the door after asking it. 'Who paid you to doctor the file?'

Hannah was aghast; she hadn't expected that question to come up when face-to-face with the man.

'I beg your pardon?' Scott stormed, face reddening almost to the colour of beetroot.

Burton was prepared for the onslaught. 'Like I said–' he began, but Scott cut him off almost instantly.

'You have a bloody cheek coming here and asking me something like that! Do you know what you're implying, son?'

'Yes, I know exactly what I'm implying, but it's a question that I have to ask. You were a detective, you know how this goes. Now can you please answer the question, or do I have to haul you down to police headquarters to answer it?'

Burton stood his ground and Hannah was very impressed at his ability to do this. The man, despite his age, looked like he could have quite easily taken a swing at Burton and knocked him straight through his living room window.

'I wasn't that kind of police officer,' he said at long last, paying heed to Burton's threat.

'So there were some who were then?'

Scott laughed. 'There are always some who are, still today I wouldn't be surprised. But no, detective, I did not doctor that report nor did anyone bribe me to do so. This is the first time I've seen it since I filed it. I'm not the one you should be looking for.'

'Do we believe him?' Hannah asked when they were in the car and driving back to the office.

'I suppose we have to,' he said reluctantly, 'although it wouldn't harm to do a little background check on him.'

'I agree. So I wonder why wasn't the boy's name in the file?' Hannah asked. 'Or the two detectives' names come to that.'

'The boy's name must have some significance if it's deliberately been removed from the file,' Burton told her. 'I'm just hoping that this is what we've been looking for.'

'I can't think how,' she told him, and he also had his doubts, but it just had to be important somehow.

Just then Burton's phone rang. When he answered it Fielding gave him the news that he'd been waiting for. The court order had arrived.

'Now, Mr Jonas Burke, time to find out exactly who you are.'

31

I t gave Joe Burton a great deal of pleasure to finally ring Jonas Burke's loyal solicitor, Mr Mark Bentley, with the news of what he was holding in his hand. As instructed by the man, Burton emailed a copy of the document to him. 'I want to examine it,' he said.

Burton sent it through and heard the solicitor's email box ping. He heard the man tut loudly upon opening the document.

'Is that all in order for you then?' Burton couldn't help the sarcasm in his voice.

Bentley was forced to agree. 'Yes,' the solicitor said with a very deep sigh that Burton assumed must be deliberately put on. 'I suppose that it is.'

'It's a court order, Mr Bentley. I trust that you are fully aware of what that means!'

'Of course I am,' the man spat back, such was his annoyance at being forced to do something that he clearly wasn't happy with.

'Well then.' Burton's patience could only be taken so far, and he always hated the power solicitors thought they had over the police.

'It's Graham ... Francis Graham. There, are you happy now?'

'And his date of birth and birthplace, please.'

'What?' Bentley seemed taken by surprise by the extra requirements.

'If you look clearly at the order, sir, you will see that it specifically requests birth name, birth date and place of birth.'

'Well, I don't know.'

'Don't know what? You don't know this information or you don't know if you can tell me?' Burton's voice was harsh. This man had been playing games with them for far too long.

'I don't know what his birth date is or where he was born.'

'Then I suggest that you get in touch with him and ask him, and then get back to me again. Today, preferably.'

'All right, all right. I'll call you back later, detective.'

And with that the sound of the phone going back on the receiver.

'He's a bit of a character!' Hannah said as Burton did the same and replaced his receiver onto its rest.

'He's a solicitor,' Burton said with contempt, 'in my experience they're all like that.'

It was while they were waiting for Bentley's call that the same thing happened with all their computers: another video popped up and started to play, but this time it was far more sinister.

'What?' Burton began, looking across at the others. From their expressions they had the same thing on their screens. This was history repeating itself.

It started off the same way as the other one had, a shaky hand-held camera in a darkened room.

'Is this the same one as before?' Fielding asked Burton, but he was too busy watching it with unblinking eyes.

Again, the backs of two chairs and again two figures were seated on them, only this time the figures on the chairs were moving.

'Oh my God!' Hannah shrieked, fearing the worst. As the camera panned around it showed two girls sitting there and not just mannequins like before.

'I warned you,' the disguised voice told them, 'I said the next time it would be for real and I wasn't kidding. If you want to make sure these children stay alive you will stop your snooping now. I will send you the details of where they are so that you can come and get them. But you've been warned.'

And with that the video ended. Hannah was already on her phone to her daughter.

'Slow down, Mum,' Amy told her when she answered the call. 'Of course I know where Millie is, she's still in school.'

'Will you ring the school and confirm that with them?'

'Why, whatever's the matter?'

'Can you just ring them and then call me back? Please, Amy!' Hannah was frantically trying to keep her emotions in check for her daughter's sake.

'Okay, I'll do that. This isn't something to do with that parcel, is it?' Amy asked her. Hannah didn't want to tell her anything as she didn't want her to become upset, so she lied.

'I was out with the car and thought I saw her, that's all.'

'Well I can tell you now, that wouldn't have been her. Like I said–'

'Amy ... please can you ring!'

'Okay, okay, I'll do it now.'

'Call me back,' Hannah insisted.

'I said that I would.' And with that she ended the call.

While Hannah was waiting for her to call back Burton rang Doris Mendelson.

'Jemima?' she asked in astonishment. 'Why she's here, detective.'

'What?'

'Yes, we've been in all day. Why are you asking?'

Burton was actually stuck for an answer, not expecting the response he'd been given.

'Is everything okay?' she asked him before he could think of anything. He now wished that he hadn't called but, under the circumstances, he had no choice but to ring her.

'Yes, everything's fine,' he blurted out, 'I'm sorry to have rung you, it was a mistake.'

'All right,' she said, a little confused. No doubt he'd be getting another furious call from her husband in due course.

'I don't understand,' he looked across the desk at his colleagues.

'I think somebody is playing with us,' Hannah spoke up. 'Amy rang me back while you were on the phone to Mrs Mendelson. My granddaughter is in school; has been all day.'

'So who were the two children in the video then?'

Before that question could be answered they received the promised follow-up from whoever had sent them the original recording. Another message popped up, but this time it was a photograph of the outside of what looked like a disused building, with a sign reading 'Radlons' on it. Burton immediately punched the name 'Radlons' into the search box, which brought up an address on the Tyne Tunnel Trading Estate.

'Quick,' he said, grabbing his coat, 'let's get going.'

As the photo suggested the factory was disused, and it was situated right at the very bottom of a road that was very much operational. Burton noticed the other units as he drove down to it: a fabric store, print shop and a computer service business.

The front door of the factory was locked when they tried it, but as they made their way around to the back of the building, they found that one of the side doors had been left ajar. As they started to go in Burton instructed the other two to turn on the torch function of their phones. His was still out of action and with the tech team. Although the light from them wasn't that great they could still see to make their way around. The inside of the building wasn't as big as the outside suggested, and seemed to be mainly open-plan office space. As there had been no indication of where the video had been shot, the only thing they could do is search until they found it.

Hannah saw the two plastic chairs first, standing in a corner and facing away from them. But even from this distance they could see that they were unoccupied. Thankfully. However, as they approached, they could see a sheet of white paper left on each of the chairs.

'What on earth is this?' Burton said, lifting up one and then the other. On the reverse side was a message, obviously intended for them. One sheet read 'NEXT' and the other read 'TIME'.

'We couldn't really see the children's faces, could we?' Fielding stated. 'We only assumed that they were the two girls. They could have been absolutely anybody; children of the bastard who made the video even. He probably told them they were playing a game.'

Burton screwed each of the sheets up into a ball and threw them away.

'What about prints?' Hannah couldn't believe what he had done.

'There'll be nothing on there,' he told her. 'These guys are professionals. Hell, we can't even get prints off that parcel that was left for you, so I'm sure there'll be nothing on them either.'

Deflated, yet ultimately relieved, Burton turned around and led them back to the car.

32

Mark Bentley may not have been Joe Burton's favourite person, but he rang them back quicker than expected and left a message when they were out of the office.

'His birthday is the fourteenth of August 1971, and he was born in Hexham,' he said sharply before the line went dead.

'Okay,' Burton said, logging on to his computer, 'let's punch this information in and see what comes back.'

Sally and Hannah stood behind him and watched as he input the name and date of birth. A lot more results came back than they could have imagined.

'How about putting a location in as well,' Hannah suggested, and Burton added Hexham to what he already had. It may have brought the numbers down, but still not to a level of his liking.

'How about looking at his birth certificate? That should give us the names of his parents.' Fielding had made a good suggestion and Burton instructed her to get onto that straight away. Working her way through a couple of the websites where you could locate past and present relatives, she finally managed to find four boys born on that date, and in the town of Hexham.

The only thing now was to figure out just which one was the right one.

She printed off all the details of each then sat scrutinising them in turn. As she was looking one thing stood out to her. For three of the four, the birth had been registered at the local registrar's office within a few days of the birth, but one of them had first been registered a long time later than that. Fifteen years later, in fact.

'That looks like a name change to me. Maybe his mother remarried and they legally changed the boy's name?'

'So if that's Burke then we still don't know his original birth name. We're no further forward!'

'It names the parents though,' Sally said.

Hannah went over to take a look, but something unusual on the sheet of paper caught her attention. 'Now that's funny,' she said looking at the printout.

'What's that?' Sally asked, curious as to what she had spotted and she had missed.

'Oh no, it's nothing,' Hannah insisted. 'It's just a coincidence, that's all. It's the parents' names; they're the names of Paul Winters's mother and father. That's a bit of a funny coincidence, don't you think?'

'I don't believe in coincidences,' Burton stated, getting up from his seat, 'especially when he's a person of interest in all this. Where was Paul born, Hannah?'

'Somewhere in Northumberland, I think. He has that slight guttural pronunciation of the letter R, which is quite common in the county. I like it, I think it's quite charming and countrified.'

Burton had noticed Winters's guttural R, he knew what it was and had also noticed it in Burke's accent and had made a mental note of it when he'd heard it. What he was more concerned about was learning exactly where in Northumberland Winters hailed from.

'What are you thinking?' Fielding asked him as she saw him, still standing, begin to quickly type something on the keyboard.

'Just a hunch,' he replied. 'Give me a minute and I'll tell you.'

Fielding and Hannah watched while his eyes darted over the pages he was bringing up until, finally, he stopped and a smile crossed his face.

'Eureka!' he cried looking over at them.

'Are you going to tell us then?' Fielding asked. Whatever he had found was apparently important, and he was more than happy to impart it to them both.

'According to Paul Winter's personnel records–'

Hannah was horrified. 'You've accessed his personnel record?'

Burton nodded, still beaming.

'But what if he finds out what you've done?' she continued, astonished by his actions. One of the big no-nos in the police force was to go into a serving officer's personnel file without due reason.

'Well I hope he does,' he continued, 'as I think I have good reason to. It appears that his parents and those of Francis Graham are one and the same, even down to their occupations.'

'So what are you implying, that Paul Winters and this Francis Graham, or Jonas Burke, are what, brothers? That's a bit of a long shot isn't it?'

'I know it is,' he said excitedly, 'but think about it. Francis Graham first appeared in the birth records on the fourteenth of August 1986, but it's stating that his age then is fifteen. Why is that do we think?' He continued before allowing anyone to offer any sort of suggestion. 'Paul Winters's records states that his father was murdered.'

Hannah let out a gasp; she had no knowledge of any of that.

'And that was in 1983,' Burton continued after giving her a quick glance. 'There's also mention of a brother.'

'That can't be!' Hannah declared. 'Why didn't he say anything to me about either of those things?'

'I suspect that the murder of his parent was not the sort of thing he wanted to talk about, Hannah,' Burton told her. 'As for his brother, there are a multitude of reasons why. Perhaps they're estranged or something?'

'But if that's the case, then it means that the young boy in the pantry all those years ago was Jonas Burke, and he is Paul Winters's brother!'

'We need to find out more about that case, Hannah, as the official records aren't showing us anything especially now that they've been doctored,' Burton told her.

'What about contacting the ambulance service?' Fielding suggested. 'The young boy was seen by a doctor, isn't that right, Hannah?' She turned to her colleague.

Hannah nodded, still reeling from what she'd heard about her friend and ex-colleague. She herself had, on DI Scott's gruff instructions, taken the boy out to see a medic, and she remembered that there was an ambulance already there to check on the boy's father – but, of course, they were too late to do anything for him. But she did hand the youngster over into the care of the ambulance staff.

'Good idea,' Burton told her. *At last*, he thought, *we might just have something concrete to go on.*

'Your medical records only go back twenty-five years?' Burton couldn't believe it. Here they were having yet another bureaucratic door slammed in their face.

'How far back are you looking to go?' The girl from North East Ambulance Service on the other end of the telephone had asked him, to which he had told her back to 1983.

'No, I'm afraid not; nobody needs records that far back.'

'Well I do!' he snapped, then proceeded a little calmer as the girl started to apologise to him. 'Can you please put me through to your supervisor then?'

The girl obviously thought that she had done something terribly wrong and Burton sensed her agitation at the thought of being reprimanded by her line manager for not being able to help him.

'Listen, it's not your fault, I'm not wanting to speak to your supervisor about you,' he told her to allay her fears, 'I just need some further information about something else while I'm on the line.'

The girl sounded relieved and said that she would put him through to the office manager, a Mr Peter Stockton.

'That's an odd request,' Stockton had said after listening to what Joe Burton had asked of him.

'It's an odd case,' Burton told him. 'If there are no records to speak of then how about the ambulance crew? Are there any still serving who were around the Hexham area in 1983?'

'Hexham in 1983 would have come under Northumbria Ambulance Service as the North East Ambulance Service Trust wasn't formed until 2006.'

'So would there be any records?' Burton was becoming impatient as this was starting to look like another dead end to him.

'The only thing I can think of,' Stockton told him after a moment's thought, 'would be word of mouth.'

'Meaning?'

'There are still some serving ambulance crew working today who might just remember who was about in the eighties. I could ask around and get some names for you?'

'Yes, that would be very helpful, if you could. Time is of the essence though.'

'Of course, I'll get on to that straight away,' Stockton told him.

Burton was delighted. Maybe not such a dead end then.

'Well that's hopeful then,' Fielding said after he told them about what Stockton had said. 'If we can locate one of the crew then he can perhaps recall what happened to the boy afterwards.'

'But it's been such a long time,' Hannah said thoughtfully. 'If they're like Martin Scott with his good memory then we've got a good chance, but if they're all like Barry Small then I don't think we'll have much luck.'

'It's all we've got, Hannah,' Burton said to her, hoping that at least one person may be able to come back to them with knowledge regarding the event. 'Scott said that the boy was memorable; did he seem that to you?'

'Not that I can recall,' she admitted. 'He was a boy, about twelve I would say, and he seemed terrified. Kept looking towards the back door if my memory serves me correctly, which made me think that he'd seen everything ... including who the killer was, if not the actual murder itself.'

'I wonder why Scott thought there was something off with him?'

'I have absolutely no idea,' Hannah told him. 'He seemed fine to me, just really shook up that's all. Knowing Scott, he probably took that shock as a sign of something else. Such a nasty, horrible man!'

Burton's mobile rang, and as he looked at it he saw that the call was Ambleton. Could this be the call that he had been waiting for? Excusing himself he left the room and walked to the end of the corridor.

'Hello, boss,' he said, and braced himself.

'I've done as you asked,' she told him, 'and the answer is no.'

'Thank goodness for that!' Burton exclaimed, relieved that he'd been wrong.

'Did you mention it to her?'

'No I didn't, thankfully. I really didn't want what I was thinking to be right on this one. Imagine if I'd mentioned it before I knew for sure.'

'Well, Joe, you can rest assured that William Fielding was never a police advisor for anyone, let alone a writer. He was as straight as a die, and that information has come directly from the top. He was certainly not someone who would divulge confidential information to anyone. Was it the letter W that was worrying you?'

'Yes, but there are now a number of people in this investigation who have the letter W in their names. But this whole case is worrying me, boss. We've just found out that Jonas Burke is Paul Winters's brother. We haven't spoken to him to confirm it, but the facts are pointing right to it.'

'What? And he hasn't mentioned it before now?'

'No, not at all.'

Ambleton whistled down the phone. 'Okay, just go carefully, and if I were you I wouldn't trust anyone.'

'Oh, I know,' he assured her before ending the conversation.

Fielding and Hannah both looked up when he re-entered the room.

'Hannah's just had an idea,' Fielding told him, and Hannah took over.

'Paul Winters is from the Northumberland area so I was wondering if he might know of anybody up that way who could help us with all this.'

'You mean the ambulance crew? But knowing what we know now, can we safely approach him?'

'Meaning what?' she asked.

'If Burke is indeed his brother, why hasn't he mentioned it

for one thing. And another, what if he's the one who is covering up for him and deleting information in the files?'

'But if that's the case,' Fielding intervened, 'then we can't let him know. We should proceed with any line of enquiry as if we didn't know who his brother is. And we should keep everything we find to ourselves.'

'A sort of double bluff you mean?' Burton asked, and she nodded.

'Okay then. If he doesn't know what we've found out, and if we don't tell him, then he can be of use to us. Hannah, Stockton said, "word of mouth", well I'm sure Paul knows a whole lot of people at the top who can get the word out for us. Do you want to give him a call and ask?'

'I'll do better than that,' she said, 'I'll go up and see him myself.'

'Be very careful then. We don't want to give anything away.'

'Don't worry, I won't.'

Fielding had had her head down working hard on something, but then suddenly leapt up from her chair with both hands in the air. Burton looked up, wondering what was happening.

'I've found him!' she declared triumphantly.

'Found who?'

'Our young Jonas Burke – the boy in the pantry!'

'How on earth did you find that?' Burton was impressed. He knew she was working frantically on something, but he wasn't exactly sure what that was.

What she had been doing was inputting all the information they knew about the case into various databases, then cross-referencing everything until a handful of results popped up. After going through each in turn, she finally found it – not in the police database, as they knew that they probably couldn't rely upon that anyway, but actually in the *Hexham Courant* newspaper. And what was even more exciting, the newspaper had a photograph of the boy.

'Bloody hell, Sally,' Burton couldn't contain his admiration of the girl. 'I could kiss you!' Then felt himself flush as he realised what he had just said.

She just looked at him and laughed, not a mocking kind of laugh but more out of relief at finding the information. She seemed to have completely missed the last part.

He pushed his chair across to hers and read what was on the screen. This find was an absolute gold mine. Not only did it have photographs of the boy and the two detectives, looking nothing like themselves thirty plus years on except, in Scott's case, his extreme height, but also photographs of the ambulance crew and doctor attending to the boy at the back of the ambulance. The article also included the house number, the street and the town.

'This is incredible,' he told her, 'more than we could have hoped for. Far more.'

But what perhaps was more important was the article named everyone in the photographs, including the boy. It confirmed that he was indeed Mark Winters, which served to reinforce what they'd only just discovered. There was also another piece of information in the story, and that was that the boy had been taken to a hospital in Stannington, Northumberland.

Y*ou do exactly as you are told and sit on the chair in the front room. A doctor examines you while your mother and the young lady police officer are there.*

You are silent. You don't utter a sound.

You hear a noise in the hallway and look towards the open door where you see two men who are dressed in black suits carry your father down the hallway in a big black bag.

You have no idea where they are taking him. Your mother tells you not to look, but it is too late. What difference will looking make now as you saw him die – something far worse than seeing him covered up in a bag, surely? But your mother is not to know that, is she?

After the examination the doctor leads you out of the house and into the parked ambulance. He takes your arm and helps you up the steps and you sit down on the seat indicated. Your father is not in there. Where have the suited men taken him?

The boy is nowhere to be seen now; he has successfully managed to flee the scene. Of course he would do that; he always does.

You are not sure where they are taking you, but you must remember to say exactly what you have rehearsed over and over in your head. You have to say what he has told you to say.

34

'Do you think that she's okay?' Fielding asked Burton after about twenty minutes had passed since Hannah's departure. He'd been collating all the evidence to send off to DCI Ambleton. Obviously, he couldn't now approach Paul Winters with what they had found. They had decided to send all the information on to her so she could take it up with the powers-that-be from there. If it was indeed the case that Winters had provided the man they now knew to be his brother with confidential information, then it needed to be handled at the highest level by someone independent and impartial. He could think of no person better to do this than DCI Ambleton.

'I think we should give Hannah a bit of space,' Burton told Fielding. He knew how it would be upsetting to her, especially as she had started the whole ball rolling on this case in the first place, 'And a bit of time. This has to be hard for her.'

'Here's a thought,' Fielding said to him. 'Do you think that we need to see the doctor's report on Mark Winters after his father's death?'

'Why, what are you thinking?' Burton was curious. He didn't

think it necessary now to know what had happened afterwards, but Fielding had obviously thought of something significant.

'I don't know,' she confessed, 'it's just bugging me, what Martin Scott said about the boy. He seemed to imply that he wasn't quite with it, which, as Hannah said, is understandable under the circumstances, but it might be beneficial to see what the report says about him.'

'Who, Scott or the boy?'

She gave him a withering look. No matter what the situation he could always find humour in it somewhere. 'You know what I mean,' she said. 'So what about the German connection? How does that fit into things?'

There are far too many unanswered questions, Burton thought. 'I have no idea,' he told her, 'but I'm sure as hell going to find out.'

'So do you think that the letter W, or the two Vs meant to look like a W, that we've been seeing could refer to Burke's brother, Paul Winters?'

'It could well do, but I think that we should leave it all here for tonight: this has been a tough day and we could do with sleeping on all this. We can start afresh in the morning.'

Sally agreed with him. 'So what about Hannah?'

'We can look for her as we leave.'

Right then the door opened and Hannah returned to the office.

'Are you okay?' Fielding asked her, and she nodded. However, she looked completely drained of colour.

'Yes, I'm fine,' she thanked Fielding for her concern, 'but that was difficult. However, I think I played it well and he says that he's going to get in touch with some people he knows up in Northumberland. Said he'll start ringing around now.'

'That's great,' Burton told her. 'We're calling it a night; we'll take a fresh look at all this in the morning after we've all had a good night's sleep and had time to dwell on all of this.'

Everyone agreed.

But what Burton and Fielding didn't know was Hannah had gone up to see Paul Winters in his office and had had a very interesting conversation with him, and not only about Northumbria Ambulance Service.

35

You wonder if this is the end; the end of all the years of feeling safe in the knowledge that nobody but one knows your secret? You trust him to keep it because you know that he won't tell.

How can he?

It can't end like this, it just can't. The other one has kept his distance, only coming to be with you when needed. He can do things that you can't; do the most heinous things that you won't. He's the person you wish you can be, do the things you need to have done, and he makes it all happen for you.

You haven't seen him in a while; will he now come to help you again?

36

'Frank Mendelson is lying to us about that van,' said Burton suddenly.

Fielding jumped at his sudden statement. 'Where did that come from?' They had been sitting, as had become their habit in the evening, in Mrs Fielding's conservatory. There had been a companionable silence up until that point, broken only by soft sounds from the Scandinavian crime drama Mrs Fielding was watching in the next room.

'I just assumed he was telling the truth when he said it wasn't his van. But I was thinking about it.' Burton took a sip of his coffee. 'You can't just change ownership details on the DVLA without solid documentary proof to accompany it.'

'Like the logbook and so on,' said Fielding thoughtfully.

'Somebody savvy enough on the inside could feasibly doctor an internal police database, but the DVLA is an entirely different matter.' He knew that the DVLA's external database was protected by firewalls and security that, he hoped, were hacker-proof. 'So, logically, Frank Mendelson has to be in on it to some degree but I'm not sure in what capacity other than "white-van owner".'

'And what about his wife?' wondered Fielding.

'Doris, I think, is just an over-enthusiastic fan – but I've got her on my list anyway.' He patted his pocket. This time his note-book was definitely there.

'You've got a list now?' Fielding teased him. 'Who else?'

'Just as a precaution those two computer techies, Lex Barker and Matt Devonshire.'

'Speaking of techies, did you get anything back about those two so-called tech experts who were rummaging around in the office the other night?'

Burton shook his head. 'The CCTV facial recognition check came back with nothing. So they're still unknown – but I haven't forgotten them.' He caught sight of his nose in dark glass of the conservatory. It looked less bruised now but it still ached when he smiled or frowned. 'Next we've got Martin Scott. I didn't like him much.'

Fielding recalled her partner's account of the former officer's less-than-caring attitude towards others, in particular, Scott's callous comments about his partner's inability to remember things the way he used to, and the language he used about the mental capacity of the young boy (now known to be the young Jonas Burke). 'He sounds like the remnant of a bygone era,' she commented. 'And if his treatment of Hannah is anything to go by, the other day as well as in the past, he is also a misogynistic boor.'

Burton was also concerned about the luxurious double-fronted house with the BMW parked on its neat gravel drive. These things shouldn't have been affordable on either a police officer's salary or pension.

'Oh, what about Alan Bedlington?' An image of Jonas Burke's researcher playing his video game popped incongruously into Fielding's head.

'No. I'm crossing him off the list. He lives too far away. And my gut says he's not involved. Look how willing he was to give us whatever information we asked for.'

'So who's at the top of your list then?'

'Paul Winters.' Just then the TV sounds changed to a theme tune and Burton decided to shut the conversation down in case Mrs Fielding started to pay attention. He glanced towards the door and gave Sally a significant look.

She got his meaning, as she usually did.

Burton was more suspicious of DCI Winters than he'd let on. They'd found him on a couple of occasions sitting in their office looking through their findings, although he hadn't been hiding that he was doing so when discovered. And now with the revelation that he was brother to the author Jonas Burke, well, Burton found that to be something that couldn't be overlooked.

There are six people on my list, he thought. *And Winters is sitting right up there at number one.*

37

Hannah couldn't sleep that night. She tossed and turned, going over and over in her head the conversation that she'd had with Paul Winters and what she'd demanded he do for her.

She hadn't expected him to agree, but he had. And now she couldn't get it out of her mind.

She got up from the bed and slid her feet into her slippers. Walking onto the landing she took the pole for the loft hatch and slipped the crooked end of it into the hook above her and tugged. It brought the hatch cover and the ladder down in one easy movement.

She knew what she needed to find and knew exactly where she would find it. It had been put up there with the rest of the mementos she'd kept from among her late husband's things. You couldn't throw something like that away.

It should really have been handed back at some point. It had been, she believed, his own father's, but perhaps he knew that one day she might have a use for it. And today was that day it seemed.

The shoebox was stacked neatly on top of a series of storage boxes and she lifted it off. It was caked with dust but she brushed it off with a sweep of her hand. Lifting the lid she removed the top layer of tissue paper and looked down. There it was, looking the same as she remembered it the day it had been put in there. Maybe a little less shiny perhaps, but that could easily be rectified with a polishing cloth and a bit of elbow grease. She took it out. It felt heavier than she remembered it to be, but she just wanted to get the feel of it before using it – as she knew that she must.

38

Hannah had been tempted to say something about Joe Burton's exhausted appearance when he walked in, but Sally Fielding had spotted her expression and mouthed 'no'. She understood from this that Burton had got himself so embroiled in this case that he would be seeing it through to the bitter end. But not, surely, at the expense of his own health.

'I've been thinking it over.'

All night, by the look of it, Hannah thought.

'...and I think what we need to do is get all of these suspects down to HQ and interview them. Put them all together in a waiting area and see if there is any reaction or recognition.'

'Well the two tech people that we already know about are already in the building, so that's two less to herd up,' Fielding astutely told him.

'And Winters,' he added.

Hannah had driven herself in today as she'd told them the previous evening that she had an appointment to go to later in the afternoon. She found it hard to concentrate on what Burton was saying as she thought about what was going to happen later. A concerned comment from Fielding made her realise that her quietness had been noted.

'Are you okay, Hannah? Didn't you get a good night's sleep either?' Fielding asked her, a little concerned at her overall demeanour.

'Not really,' Hannah said, 'I had a lot to think about.' She left it at that. Closing conversations off is a useful skill for a detective, and Hannah had honed it over the years. Fielding had the good sense not to waste time and energy pursuing the matter.

'I'm determined to get to the bottom of this whole business today,' Burton continued. 'We're not having this hanging over us any longer. It needs to be sorted out now right now!'

'Do you want me to contact everybody and get them in for this afternoon?' Fielding asked Burton. He appeared to be buzzing now that he'd quickly downed a cup of freshly brewed coffee and was helping himself to another.

'Yes, please, if you don't mind.'

Hannah's phone pinged and she picked it up off the desk and looked at it.

'Just reminding me of my appointment at 6pm,' she told them. But it wasn't a reminder for an appointment. It was the text message from Paul Winters that he'd promised to send her when they spoke the previous day. Everything was arranged for six o'clock, but he did not disclose the meeting place. He'd told her to come to his office and they would drive down there together.

The stage was set, and she would finally get the chance to set things right. And she had just what she needed to do that in the boot of her car.

In Joe Burton's mind giving four hours' notice to attend an interview at police headquarters was a very reasonable request. So when he met opposition from Frank Mendelson he wasn't prepared to stand for any nonsense.

'Look, Mr Mendelson,' he had boomed down the phone, making both Hannah and Sally look up from what they were doing, 'this is an official police request for you to attend, so any reluctance to do so will result in your arrest. Do I make myself clear?'

'Perfectly,' Mendelson had responded. He had not expected such an outburst.

'Good. Then I will see you at 3.30 ... on the dot.'

Everybody else had agreed without any fuss, including the two tech experts, and it had only been Mendelson who had initially proved difficult. *He's got something to hide*, thought Burton. Whether or not it was true, he hoped to find out later in the afternoon.

But then, of course, there was the great man himself, Jonas Burke, to contact again. As he was a prominent feature in all this, they wished to interview him in a police station this time and not just happen across him whilst he was giving one of his book talks or signings. Even though he had the man's mobile number, Burton rang his agent Douglas Langley again out of courtesy, and was very surprised with the response.

'Mr Burke should be up in the north east by now,' Langley told him.

'Oh?' Burton asked, 'for what purpose?' He assumed the answer would be yet another book-signing for his hordes of loyal and trusty fans.

'His tour has now ended so he'll be back home again getting started, I hope, on his next novel,' came the response.

'And back home being?'

'Why, Hexham, of course. That's not far from where you are, isn't it? I assumed that you knew.'

Burton couldn't believe what he was hearing. How had Burke's home address not come up in the conversation before now? Okay, they now knew that he had been born in Hexham, but had no idea that he was still living up in Northumberland. Why had everyone assumed, himself included, that Burke lived in or near London?

'You won't believe this!' Burton declared after finishing his call to Douglas Langley and had obtained the author's address. Hannah and Fielding turned to face him. 'Jonas Burke lives in Hexham!'

'He lives where?' Fielding was as bewildered as Burton was upon first hearing it. 'Well we need to get him down here as soon as possible.'

'We'll have to do it tomorrow as we now have all these people coming in this afternoon,' Burton told her.

'So you have his address?'

'Yes, Langley gave it to me.'

Was my reaction to that information right? wondered Hannah, as she noticed Fielding looking at her oddly. *Should I have looked more surprised?* Hannah put her head down and got on with her work, hoping to head off any questions.

But the younger woman was not going to let it go, it seemed. Halfway through the morning she brought Hannah a cup of tea and rolled her chair over to the desk and said, 'You sure you're okay? You look as if you have the weight of the world on your shoulders.'

Hannah almost broke at that moment, but she couldn't allow herself to do that now. Things had moved forward quickly, and this was something that she had to see through to the end herself. So she simply made light of the situation by saying that she didn't care for the doctor that she had an appointment with that evening and left it at that. Which, in fact, wasn't entirely a lie – apart from the doctor part.

39

Joe Burton was so convinced that he was going to solve this case today that he started tidying up his work-station.

'You seem very sure that one of these people is the cause of the leaked data,' Fielding said to him.

'Yes, I am. Why, aren't you?' He seemed to have it all done and dusted in his mind and was surprised that his partner didn't seem as convinced as he was. 'They're all involved, especially Winters: he is Burke's secret sibling after all.'

'I'm hoping so, but I'm not at the stage of desk-tidying yet,' she told him, however, she was concerned about the Winters–Burke relationship.

'It doesn't mean that Paul's involved, you know.' Hannah spoke up after being silent for so long, sensing, perhaps, what was going through both Burton's and Fielding's minds. 'He's never mentioned in the past that he even had a brother, let alone that he's a world-famous author.'

'But why wouldn't he,' Burton asked her, 'unless there's something amiss?'

'Perhaps they were never close in the first place, or maybe

they fell out with one another at some point. Families do fall out, you know.'

Burton was beginning to doubt if it was a good thing that Hannah was even there. Perhaps, under the circumstances, it would be better to detach her from the case entirely.

'Look, Hannah–' he began, but she anticipated what he was going to say and stopped him.

'I know what you're thinking and I want to stick with this to the end, if you'll let me that is.'

'Well only if you're sure. I know that this is hard for you. I know that we're not entirely certain of Paul's involvement in this, but you have to admit that it's not looking too good, especially as we now know that he's related to the man.'

'But it doesn't mean that he's the one who leaked all the information,' she insisted.

'That's true, but we need to find out for certain, and these people who are coming in this afternoon are the only ones who have any sort of link to it. We'll find out what we can today and then get Burke to come in tomorrow to finally sort it out once and for all.'

'I'm sure that he'll want his legal representative present,' Fielding told him, 'so you'd better get in touch with him and, if he insists, his solicitor, today.'

'Yes, I'll do that now.' He noticed a new-found firmness in Fielding's voice; an urgency, it seemed, to get all of this sorted out and behind her. *It can't be easy to have something like this hanging over you*, he thought. He knew that this was what she wanted, and that was why he'd wanted so much to help her from the start. Perhaps seeing him tidy his desk gave her renewed hope that closure was coming. He felt as if they were now at the final hurdle.

However, they still had some way to go yet.

Burton hoped that the report from hospital would come through before the afternoon's gathering of suspects. What Martin Scott had said spurred him into action on this line of enquiry. He had said that there was something off with the boy, so what had the attending doctor's take been?

With a little digging Burton had found out where young Mark Winters had been taken following the incident at his home. He had contacted the hospital in Stannington, Northumberland, to gain access to the records, but because of the length of time since his admission they had all been archived.

'Right,' Burton had said to the secretary. 'I am requesting voluntary disclosure under Section 29 of the Data Protection Act.' He had stressed that his need for the information in the notes was crucial to their current enquiry and she had been extremely co-operative.

'Email your request and I'll send the copy over as soon as I can retrieve them,' she had said briskly.

So Burton was forced to put his hope in her and sent off the request by email, stressing once again for good measure that time was of the essence.

Just after 3pm the suspects began to arrive. The reception desk had called up to say that the first ones had just signed in, and it was then that Burton positioned himself on the first floor mezzanine so he could watch them as they entered the building.

The security guard had been told to get them to sit in reception as soon as they came in. 'I'll come and get them once they've all arrived,' said Burton.

The first to arrive were the Mendelsons. You can tell just by looking at someone that they are annoyed, and the vexation on the husband's face said it all; it was a perfect portrayal of the displeasure of having been asked to come in. His wife, on the other hand, just looked plain terrified. Burton wasn't sure if that was through guilt, fear of her husband, or even the fear of being called into police headquarters, but she certainly didn't look too comfortable.

After about five or so minutes had passed Martin Scott walked through the door. He approached the desk and was told to sit down with the others. Burton watched closely as the former detective cast a quick glance over those waiting.

He had also asked the two tech people, Lex and Matt, to come down to reception. Again, he needed to see if there was any initial recognition from those already seated.

As for Paul Winters, Burton planned to have a word with him privately after the interviews, although he was going to mention his name in passing to each of the interviewees to see how they reacted. So by 3.30pm all the players were in place, but none appeared to recognise any of the others, or if they did they were keeping it to themselves. At which point Burton descended the stairs to meet them.

40

First into the interview room was Doris Mendelson.

'I really don't know what else I can tell you,' she told Burton and Fielding as she sat down. They had agreed that Hannah would remain in the adjoining room with the others.

'Well for one thing, tell me about your black eye.'

Doris put one hand up to the eye in question. The bruising was now practically gone and only a small trace of yellow surrounded the area. 'I told you how that happened,' she insisted.

But Burton now knew for certain that she hadn't simply fallen over one of her daughter's toys and challenged her on that.

'You're lying, Mrs Mendelson,' Burton said more firmly.

She started to protest but he continued. 'You know how I know, because the person who gave you that black eye also knocked me out and gave me a bloody nose.'

She gasped and looked at his face, then looked frantically around the room.

'They could be watching me now,' she whispered, having found what she was looking for.

Fielding followed her eyes up to the camera mounted on the wall. 'There's nobody watching you; it isn't turned on,' she assured her.

'Are you certain?'

'Yes, there's no red light on.'

Doris Mendelson scrutinised it closely then hung her shoulders in despair. There was no use her hiding it from them now as they knew, and it felt like a weight had been lifted from her.

'They threatened me,' she began. 'When they came to the door and said that Mr Burke had sent them I thought how nice, thinking that he'd sent them to see my collection. But when they were in the house they turned nasty. Told me to stop sharing information about him with you because he was angry that I'd done so. I couldn't see what harm I'd done but then they threatened my daughter, and it was then that I took it seriously. The man punched me in the face, saying that was a warning for me and that worse would happen if I gave you any more information.'

'So they weren't wearing masks?' Burton asked her.

'No. I wouldn't have let them in the house if they had been. I'm not that daft.'

Burton took the photo out of a folder and put it in front of her. 'Were these the two people who came to your house?'

Doris looked closely at the photo taken from the CCTV footage in the reception area.

'They could be. Yes, I think that they are.' She handed it back to him.

Burton felt sorry for the woman. Through no fault of her own she had been dragged into this mess and her only crime, it seemed to him, was being a fan of the author.

Before closing the interview he asked the question he intended to ask everyone. 'And how do you know Paul Winters?'

'Who?' she responded, looking genuinely blank, so there was no need in Burton's mind to proceed any further with that line of questioning.

Sadly, they didn't have any more luck with Frank Mendelson, who came in, sat down and immediately reprimanded them about the way they had treated his wife and, as expected, Burton's recent telephone call about his child.

'Now just wait a minute,' Burton began. He certainly wasn't going to put up with anything like that from a suspect.

Fielding jumped in as it looked like it might turn heated.

'We didn't ask your wife anything untoward,' she informed him. 'We only asked her about the black eye and about your van. And as for the phone call, we had reason to worry about Jemima's safety.'

Both Burton and Fielding could see the man was fast approaching boiling point, but he managed to successfully keep it together to respond to her. 'I have told you before.' His words were slow and precise and directed only at Fielding. Perhaps he feared that if he looked at Burton he may be tempted to strike out at him. 'My wife hit her eye when she tripped and fell. And as for that bloody white van, let me tell you – yet again – I have never owned, and I never will own a white van.'

'But the DVLA–'

'Sod the bloody DVLA. I'm not exactly sure what is going on here or what this is all about, but somebody has somehow fixed that to make it look like I've done something wrong.'

At that point Mendelson rose from the chair, put both hands on the table palms down, and glared at the two detectives. 'Now, if you're not going to charge either my wife or myself with anything – and I can't possibly think that you are as neither of us have done anything wrong – then are we free to go?'

Burton and Fielding exchanged glances. Burton said heavily, 'Yes, you are free to go.'

But as the angry man turned to go Burton raised the Paul Winters question.

'I've no idea who that is,' Mendelson stated as he walked through the door, not even turning around to face them.

When he had left the room Fielding let out a long breath. 'Do we believe him?' she asked.

'If he's faking it then he's doing a very good job of it. I'm really not sure about him. But let's make him think that he's out of the woods while keeping an eye on him. Maybe the two techies will be more helpful. After all, all that business with the disappearing video and database modifications, they're more likely to be responsible for that than a guy working in banking.'

'But didn't you say that he works in the bank's tech department?'

Burton hadn't thought of that; he just assumed that Mendelson was a team leader, nothing more, but Fielding could have a point. He was beginning to think that he'd started to tidy his desk a shade too early.

'The two techies seem too obvious to me,' she continued, 'but maybe that's what whoever is behind this wants us to think.'

'I wonder if Paul Winters is tech-minded?' Burton pondered. 'After all, we now know him to be Burke's brother – sorry I still can't call the man Mark Winters. Maybe he's been doing all the changes to the databases. Remember, we found him in the office a few times when we weren't in and he was looking through our notes. Then there's also the two unknowns who posed as techies to rummage through the office the other night. Maybe they're doing Winters's bidding and he'd arranged to get them passes and false IDs to get them into the building?'

Burton's mind was clicking over far too quickly. He desperately wanted to get this all sorted, but the more he thought he knew the more he found out that he didn't.

'Then there's the whole German connection,' he continued. 'I don't think it's random, but what on earth do we have that's related to that apart from the name Mendelson?'

'I don't know,' Fielding told him, 'but let's get either Matt or Lex in–'

'Is a Lexus car German?'

'No, it's Japanese.'

Burton looked at her questioningly. 'And how do you know that little titbit of information?'

'I looked it up after we were talking about her being named after a car.'

Good old Fielding, he thought. 'Right, let's get her in then–'

'Wait a minute,' Fielding interrupted, 'didn't we learn that Burke studied computer science at university?'

'Dammit, I forgot that!' Burton exclaimed. 'Yes, I believe we did. But surely he wouldn't have learned computer hacking there, for goodness sake?'

'No, I shouldn't have thought so,' she agreed, adding, with more than a touch of sarcasm, 'and as far as I'm aware it's not on the curriculum. But that's not what I meant; wouldn't he have met talented undergraduates perhaps savvy enough to know how. Maybe he's kept in touch with them over the years and paid them a hefty sum to do a little bit of work for him from time to time?'

'That's a distinct possibility,' Burton told her, jotting it down in his notebook.

When Lex Barker entered the room next Burton opened the conversation with a very blunt question. 'If I were to ask you to go into the police database and erase or amend a record would you be able to do it?'

'I beg your pardon?' she said to him, wondering what he was asking her to do.

'Could you feasibly do it?'

She looked at Burton and then to Fielding, hoping for some sort of an explanation. Unfortunately for her, none was forthcoming. The two detectives sat with emotionless expressions.

'It's possible,' she said, 'but I don't understand what you're asking.'

'It's a simple question, Ms Barker,' he said to her. 'Is it easy to do?'

'Well, yes, but it would leave a digital trail. Anybody who knows anything about tech knows that.'

'You mean like you couldn't find the origin of the video on my computer recently?'

'We did find it eventually, well Matt did, but finding the origin of a programme is different to trying to cover over a database change.' Again, a furtive glance between the two detectives. 'Look, I'm really not sure what you're getting at here. Has there been a computer breach or something?'

'Why do you ask that?' Fielding spoke.

'From what you're saying about removing or amending a record, that's a breach. If there has been then the department needs to know about it so that we can rectify it immediately.'

Lex answered the questions in such a way that Burton felt inclined to leave the cross-examination there. From what she'd said, his gut feeling was telling him that she was completely in the dark about any fraudulent activity surrounding the police records.

'It's nothing at all for the department to worry about,' he said to her in a much different tone. 'We were just wondering how easy it would be to do such a thing, and you've confirmed to us that it isn't easy at all. I'm sorry if it came across as an accusation in any way, but we've been told to make a stringent check.'

The girl seemed genuinely relieved. Perhaps relieved in the knowledge that her department wouldn't have to do a stringent in-depth system-wide check, a task which would take a considerable amount of time. It was at that point that Burton produced the security footage photo of the two so-called tech people from the other evening.

'Have you seen either of these two people before?' he asked her.

Taking the photo from him she scrutinised it carefully. 'I have,' she told him. 'They said that they were asked to come in from another division to check the firewalls that we have in place. I think I only saw them a couple of times but I know that Matt had quite a bit to do with them over the past week or so.'

Burton exchanged glances with his partner. She'd known him long enough to know what that look meant. 'Okay, thank you, Lex, that's been very helpful.' The question about Paul Winters was not asked for obvious reasons, and the same would apply to Matt Devonshire when it was his turn to be interviewed.

'I haven't got Matt into trouble or anything?' she asked with concern.

'No, no,' he reassured her, 'nothing like that, and it's nothing whatsoever to worry about,' and gave her the broadest smile that he could to reassure her. 'If you'd like to ask Matt to come in when you return next door, please?'

Fielding, however, thought that his smile was a bit too wide for comfort. Fortunately, Lex hadn't seemed to notice.

'What was that?' Fielding asked him as soon as the girl walked out of the door.

'What was what?' Burton appeared completely oblivious as to what had instigated the question.

'That smile was enough to frighten the poor girl. Thank goodness she didn't really see it!'

'Was it really that bad?'

'Well it frightened me!'

The gentle rap on the door announced the arrival of Matt Devonshire.

As soon as Devonshire was seated Burton asked him the same question that he'd asked Lex, and it was met with the exact same reaction. The man appeared to be horrified at the suggestion of a possible breach and the implication of it, which made Burton likewise believe his innocence in the matter.

Reassuring Devonshire that it was simply a hypothetical security question, he went on to show him the same photographs that he'd showed Lex.

'Oh yes,' he said immediately, 'they were the two who came in from Cumbria to check our firewalls.'

'Was there a problem with the firewalls that instigated their visit?' Burton asked.

'Why... no, but they said that they'd been instructed to visit each police force just to make sure that everyone was safe. I'd heard rumours over the past few weeks that the entire system was upgrading to a different server; I just naturally assumed that it was something to do with that.'

'And did their credentials seem okay to you?' Fielding asked him.

'What do you mean?' The man appeared confused.

'Did either yourself or the head of department contact Cumbria to confirm it?'

Devonshire had to think about it. 'Well, the head of department must have organised it otherwise why would they have been here?'

Why indeed? thought Burton. Other than to do a bit of dodgy database manipulation!

'Who is the head of department?' Burton asked, notebook and pen at the ready.

Matt explained that the head of IT was away on holiday and her deputy was in charge for now.

'Okay, Matt, thank you for all your help.'

'No problem,' Matt said in an upbeat way that made Burton believe that, like Lex before him, he likewise had nothing to hide.

'Well that only leaves Paul Winters,' Fielding said to Burton when the door closed. 'We'll just come out and ask him straight. He doesn't know the full extent of what we know, that he and Burke are brothers, so we'll have the element of surprise on our side. Hopefully, it will catch him unawares.'

41

'That's ... that's Hannah in there,' whispered Fielding astonished.

They had arrived at Winters's office out of breath after a sprint up the stairs. Burton had been just about to knock when he realised, from the raised voices they could hear in the office, that Winters was involved in an angry conversation with Hannah Sanderson.

'But she said she had a doctor's appointment,' whispered Burton.

'What on earth is going on?' Fielding whispered in Burton's ear, after straining to hear what was being said. But she couldn't catch much apart from the mutual anger in their voices.

Then it seemed he moved closer to the door. 'I told him that we'd both be there at six,' they heard him say.

Hannah responded, her voice louder now, 'I said I wanted to speak to him alone.'

'Not going to happen, Hannah.'

'Why can't I see him alone? Why are you protecting him; exactly what kind of hold does he have on you, Paul?'

'I'm not protecting him and he certainly doesn't have any

kind of hold on me!' Winters strongly protested. 'For heaven's sake, Hannah, I hardly know the man.'

'It sounds to me like they're talking about his brother,' Burton also spoke in a whisper. 'But did he just say that he hardly knew him? I think we should follow them as it sounds as if they are going to a meet him somewhere and I don't think it's going to be here at headquarters.'

'Why didn't she tell us what she was going to do?' Fielding asked. She'd thought that they'd all become quite the close-knit little team over the course of the investigation. So in that case, why had Hannah kept this so secret?

'We don't have time to go and get a tracker to put on Hannah's car, do we?' Fielding asked.

'No, I wouldn't think so,' he confirmed, 'although, what about tracking her phone?'

'Is that something I can do at short notice without involving the tech department?'

'I don't see why not. We've got her number so it should be a relatively easy thing to do. Get your phone out and check to see how to do it.'

Doing as she was told, Fielding retrieved her mobile from her pocket and did a search. Surprisingly enough, the results were extensive, and she was taken aback at how easy the whole process was. In fact, anybody could do it, even a not-so-tech-savvy youngster by the looks of it. That fact frightened her somewhat as it meant anybody could be traced by another person registering their mobile then pressing the 'find my device' option and, hey presto, they knew where they were – as long as their phone was turned on, that is. It was all far too easy to do in her opinion, but at that moment she was grateful for its simplicity.

Quickly inputting all the information that she needed to, Fielding had the trace set up within a matter of minutes, certainly long before Hannah walked briskly out of the office with Paul Winters following not far behind her. The programme was highly accurate, and showed exactly where Hannah was.

'Good,' Burton said, watching the pulsing red dot on his partner's phone, 'that means that we don't have to tail them too closely. I'd hate for them to spot us and call the whole thing off, whatever it is that's going down.'

'Let's hope she doesn't turn her phone off, then,' Fielding said.

Making sure that they kept a considerable distance between themselves and Hannah's car, they followed it onto the A19 and then south towards the Tyne Tunnel.

'Where are they heading?' Fielding asked whilst looking in her purse for some change for the toll.

'I don't know but I suspect that we'll soon find out.'

'You know it's funny,' Fielding began, 'but I had the idea that Burke was from down south somewhere.'

'Like me, you mean?' Burton asked, putting on a broad cockney accent.

'You don't have a noticeable accent, but yes, I suppose so; he doesn't have a strong Northumbrian accent at all.'

'So you assumed that he was from London?'

Fielding laughed. 'The big north–south divide, eh? If he's not from the north then it stands to reason that he's from the south because, as we all know, there's nothing at all in between!'

When they pulled up at the toll Fielding handed him the money to get them through the barrier and he slid down his window and put it into the machine. They'd now lost sight of Hannah's car, but the flashing red light on Fielding's phone was clearly showing where they were, and at this point they had just emerged on the other side of the tunnel.

'I hope we're not heading off down the A1 somewhere,' Burton said, checking the fuel level on the car. He'd forgotten to fill up that morning and the indicator was just below quarter full.

'Hannah said that the meeting was at six,' she told him, 'and it's nearly that now, so I don't think that they'll be going too far, and definitely not to Burke's home in Hexham as that's in the other direction.'

As Burton continued driving Fielding kept her eyes fixed on her phone, and when the flashing red indicator took the first exit off Testo's roundabout about ten minutes later she informed Burton of the change in direction. 'They've turned off to the left,' she declared, 'and it looks like they're heading to Boldon.'

Burton's phone rang and he saw a withheld number on the car's dashboard. As he was still expecting the report from Stannington he answered in the hope that this was what he was waiting for. The secretary he'd spoken to earlier said that she was sending him an email now which contained the file he'd requested. Eager to see its contents, Burton thanked her for her valued assistance and ended the call.

As they kept driving the flashing red dot finally came to a stop, and it was in the car park of a hotel in Boldon Business Park. Fielding felt a chill go through her body as she recalled what Hannah had told her on their first meeting. This is where she and her father had chased a serial killer all those years ago, and it was the hotel in which her father had died after being tasered.

42

When Hannah had made her excuses to Burton and Fielding, saying that she was going to an appointment, she left the room and went immediately upstairs to Paul Winters's office.

'I'll tell you where to go when we get in the car,' he'd told her, and she hadn't been very happy about it as she felt that he was trying to stall the meeting somehow.

'I hope you've arranged everything,' she'd said angrily. She hadn't come this far to be fobbed off and certainly wasn't afraid to make her feelings known. She was angry at the situation, angry that she'd had to cut Burton and Fielding out of this, and, if she were honest, a little scared, too. But she knew that this was something that she had to do for herself – to make things right in her mind. Not only was she doing this for herself, she was doing it for Sally as well, to find out exactly what had taken place that fateful day.

When Paul instructed her to pull into the Hotel Arcadia car park in Boldon she felt sick to her stomach. Had he done this on purpose, to bring her to this place again after all this time? She gave him a sideways look, but he was staring out of the window with his face turned away from her. Whether that was intention or not she wasn't sure.

'Why here?' she asked.

'What?'

'Why come here?' she repeated the question.

'Not my idea,' he told her, 'I was given the location. I'm not too familiar with this area.'

Unfortunately, I am, Hannah thought. After all, it was where William Fielding had met his death. *Did he really not know that or was this some sort of sick joke?*

Winters's phone pinged. 'We have to go inside,' he told her after reading the message he'd just received and opened the car door to get out. Hannah followed his lead, but not before saying that she needed to get something out of the boot.

She felt uncomfortable being in this place again. It had been redecorated, she noticed, and then wondered, why on earth she'd noticed that at this moment. She followed Winters through the automatic doors as he made his way to the reception area.

Fielding moved to get out of the car as soon as it stopped, but Burton said that he needed to read the email that had been sent through from Stannington Hospital before going in.

'What's wrong?' she asked as she saw the look on his face whilst reading it.

'It's the report,' he told her, handing the phone over to her. 'Read the summary at the end.'

Fielding took the phone. She was anxious to follow Hannah and Paul Winters, but Burton had deemed it urgent that she stop and read what had disturbed him so much in the message.

'Bloody hell!' she said when she'd read it.

Burton already had the car door open. 'If he's in there with Hannah then we'd better get in there fast.'

They both sprinted across the car park and through the automatic doors. The noise of their shoes running across the marble tiled floor made the receptionist look up from the computer monitor she was sitting behind. People didn't usually run in the foyer of Hotel Arcadia. She opened her mouth to speak to them about it when Burton and Fielding produced their warrant cards.

'Have two people come in, an older woman and a man in a suit?'

'What's this about–' she started and then thought better of it and said, 'They've gone through to the swimming pool. They said they were meeting someone there.'

Burton looked around him wondering where on earth the pool was.

The receptionist said, 'It's back out of the main entrance and then take a right turn; the door to the leisure area is just past there.'

Burton thanked her as he and Fielding sprinted back along the foyer and out the same way that they'd come in.

The place was in semi-darkness and, hardly surprising, there was nobody in the pool or lounging at the poolside. After all, it was a cold evening at the end of November with Christmas only a few weeks away. But voices echoed from around a corner at the top end of the room.

Burton put a finger up to his lips and Fielding nodded. Cautiously, they edged their way closer to try and hear what was being said and, perhaps more importantly, to find out who Hannah and Winters were meeting with. When they were as close as they dare go they stopped and listened.

Hannah was arguing with somebody, not Paul Winters, but another male voice. At first they didn't recognise it but, as they listened a little closer, they could tell that it was that of Jonas Burke, or Mark Winters. However, his voice seemed different from how it was when they'd heard him speak last.

'Oh no,' Burton whispered. 'Are you thinking what I'm thinking, bearing in mind what we've both just read?'

'If that's the case then Hannah is not safe. What should we do?'

But before Burton could answer he heard Paul Winters call out. 'Hannah! Hannah, what the hell are you doing? Where on earth did you get that gun from?'

'Did he say "gun"?' Fielding said out loud, at which point the shouting stopped, and she could almost picture them turning around as one to see who was there around the corner.

'Shit!' she said, at which point Burton decided to make a move. Hannah was in danger and he needed to do what he had to in order to protect her.

'What are you doing?' Fielding grabbed him by the arm as he moved forward, trying to stop him. 'We need to get back-up first. You can't do this without it.'

'They won't be here quick enough, I've got to do this.'

'Well let me come with you.'

'No, you ring for help; I'll try to talk them down.'

'Are you sure?' Fielding was very concerned for his safety, although she trusted that he knew what he was doing.

'I'll be fine, now go! Hurry.'

As Fielding moved further down towards the entrance to make the call, Burton moved closer to the people around the corner, and what he saw shocked him. Jonas Burke had Hannah in a headlock facing away from him as he tried to get the gun from her hand. His brother stood staring, either through fear or shock or both.

You are helpless as you watch the other take over; you can only do his bidding.

He is putting things into your mouth and you are saying them ... as he has always done. He has made you kill people; he is trying to make you kill now and you are helpless to stop him.

All you can do is watch from the distance, and breathe in the aroma of chlorine from the swimming pool.

Burke spun around at the sound of someone behind him, dragging Hannah with him. 'Ah, Detective Burton. Do come and join us all!'

'Quick, Paul,' Burton shouted, 'if we both make a move we can bring him down.'

'He's got hold of the gun,' Winters shouted, finally finding a voice.

'Yes, I'm holding the gun now and I'm not afraid to use it.' Burke placed a finger over Hannah's while she still had hers on the trigger; he was making her press down on it.

She sensed what he was about to do and cried out, 'It's okay, Joe, the safety catch is on!'

Burton moved forwards, both hands in the air showing the man that he didn't have a weapon. Burke, however, on hearing Hannah's remark about the safety, loosened his hold on her and undid the safety catch with his free hand. His brother even moved forward at that point, stirred into action to try and grab Hannah away and tackle the man to the ground. But too late. Burke squeezed her hand even tighter on the trigger, forcing the gun to go off. Joe Burton felt a sudden, searing pain through his right side, then a warm sensation around that area. He put a hand down to his side to feel where the heat was coming from then lifted it up to look at it; it was covered in bright red, sticky blood. He felt light-headed and took a few steps backwards, lost his footing and found himself falling backwards into the pool.

The water felt surprisingly warm – or was that the warmth he felt from the blood which was now circling his body. He couldn't move his hands or feet to try to swim to the side, and he felt himself slowly sinking. Soon all he could see was water above him and the wavering shapes of people standing watching him descend. Why were they just watching him? Why weren't they trying to get him out? He tried to hold his breath, but he knew that he was sinking to the bottom and there was nothing he could do about it. Strangely enough he didn't feel afraid; he didn't feel anything. Something or someone dived into the pool, but then darkness encompassed him and he lost consciousness.

43

After Joe Burton had been shot everything seemed to happen in slow motion. He sank into the pool with such elegance and grace that it would have surely warranted scores of ten from a panel of diving judges. On hearing the shot, Sally ran back to the poolside only to see him disappear into the water. She didn't give a second thought to Burke, his brother, or Hannah. All she could think about was diving into the pool to save her partner from drowning – if he hadn't already succumbed to the bullet, that is. The horror of hearing the gun going off and then the sight of the blood patch on Burton's shirt growing by the second sent her adrenaline soaring. Although by no means a good swimmer, she was not going to let that stop her from saving him.

By the time she reached him near the bottom of the pool Burton's eyes were closed and the water had turned a frightening shade of red. Using all the strength she could muster, she grabbed hold of the belt on his trousers and held on as tight she could, dragging him along with her. She could see the ladder out of the pool off to her right, and she managed to manoeuvre him over to that.

Paul Winters was waiting for her. 'Ambulance is on its way,' he said. He crouched down and reached down into the water, sliding both arms under Burton's armpits to haul him up. Once he had Burton out of the water he put a finger on Burton's neck to feel for his pulse.

He looked at Fielding, shook his head and began CPR. Hannah was standing nearby, shaking like a leaf, and still shocked that the weapon she'd brought along with her had caused this damage. Burke, however, was nowhere to be seen.

No matter, Fielding thought, *the police and ambulance are on their way, and we've got his home address*. Burke was not her priority at that moment. She was more far more concerned about Burton at that point, and anxiously watched as Winters worked on him. Eventually, and to her great relief, after a few spluttering sounds his eyelids fluttered open and a small fountain of water spouted out from his mouth. Relief washed over her.

You see your chance and you take it. In all the confusion it is not diffi-cult for you to make your escape. You are soon away from the humid pool area and into the sharp chill outside. You throw yourself into your car, turn on the ignition and go.

The other has struck again and has left you on your own to face the music, but you have to get away to somewhere safe – to hide from them and to hide from him.

Why did he grab that woman like that and make her pull the trig-ger? Did he kill somebody ... again?

Why won't he leave you alone to get on with your life? Why does he have to share yours like this? You are sick of it. His presence might supply you with fodder for your stories, but this is too much. Far too much for you to bear.

After the ambulance had arrived and Burton had been rushed away to hospital, Fielding insisted that the other two accompany her to Burke's house in Hexham. Hannah and her gun would have to be dealt with later. She'd programmed his address into her phone and was ready to follow directions. Winters was confused, as it appeared that he had no idea where his brother was living let alone that he was back home where his roots were.

'How long has he been here?' Winters asked when seated in the car.

'His agent said he'd just travelled up today to start work on a new book,' replied Fielding.

'I had no idea; we don't contact one another, you know,' he told her as if to make her more aware of his ignorance.

'When was the last time you saw him?' Fielding asked.

Winters let out a long breath, trying to remember. 'Oh, it was after the incident with our father, so quite a few decades have passed.'

'So were you living at home at that time?' Hannah tried to remember how many years had passed since the boy in the pantry murder.

'No, I'd moved out by then. I was twenty and Mark was twelve; and he was a young twelve, not like the worldly-wise twelve-year-olds of today. I'd already joined the police force and had a place of my own, but after what happened, well, I just couldn't bring myself to speak to him again and I completely disassociated myself from him. It destroyed our mother, and she was never the same person after that.'

'I've just seen the report from Stannington,' she told him, 'and it said that he had a condition.'

Hannah had been sitting in the back quiet, listening to the

conversation but, at that point, felt obliged to ask the question. 'And what kind of condition was that?'

'They concluded that he has what was then called multiple personality disorder. It's known as dissociative identity disorder today. They reckoned he himself had killed his father. It wasn't some intruder as he'd stated.'

'That's why I just couldn't get in touch with him again,' Winters said flatly.

Dissociative identity disorder is a condition characterised by at least two distinct personalities, each of whom have different emotions and reactions. It is often caused by a period of abuse. The abused creates another personality – known as an alter – and takes themselves out of the situation. This makes the person with the condition feel like another individual who has not experienced the abuse.

Mark Winters, the report stated, had created at least one other person in his mind who could handle the situation to the extent that he would kill to protect himself.

The psychologist who examined the boy said that he seemed to have created a person whom he believed he could see, and who spoke to him telling him to do as he told him – and most of that was to simply watch him taking revenge for him. The report went on to say that whilst under their care Mark did show signs of improvement in that he acknowledged the condition and came to understand that the boy he was seeing was only someone he had created in his mind. The psychiatrists concluded that, with the appropriate medication, his condition could be controlled.

He was released from Stannington and put into care as his mother didn't want anything further to do with him. The report only mentioned care within Northumbria Health Authority with no specific details.

'I knew that he'd gone to Stannington,' Winters confirmed, 'but after that, no. Neither my mother nor I mentioned it again. I guess that we thought that if we didn't discuss it then it wouldn't bring back the bad memory of it all.'

'So had he been abused at all?' Fielding had to ask the question.

'Not to my knowledge; my father had certainly not abused me when I was young, and my mother also claimed to know nothing about it. Although, I suppose, you can never tell. Mark didn't say anything to either of us, so we just assumed that it was part of his "condition", as the doctors called it.'

'We'll just have to ask him when we get to his house.'

'Are you sure he'll have gone there?' Hannah asked, her voice shaky.

Fielding looked at her in the rear-view mirror. Hannah looked pale from what she'd just witnessed, and who could blame her.

Concerned as she was by Burton's gunshot wound, Fielding knew that he was in good hands; and she could almost hear him saying to her, in typical Burton-style, to leave him, he'd be fine and to go catch the bad guy – which was something she was now determined to do. 'He can't know that we have his address, and it's the only thing I can think of. It's worth a try as it's all we really have right now.'

44

The journey to Hexham took less than an hour, and Fielding pulled into a street next to the one Burke's house was in. She still couldn't think of him as Mark Winters. It was a long time since she'd been to Hexham, not since she was a teen. But she remembered quite clearly her visit to the abbey to gather information on a school project. She'd been very impressed by its architecture.

She was also impressed by Burke's house when she spotted it. A large, modern building, it stood out from the rest and was the only one like it on the street. He was home: the place was lit up like a Christmas tree, so he evidently hadn't expected anyone to have followed him. His agent hadn't warned him that the police now knew where he lived.

Fielding was wondering which side of him had she seen by the pool. Had he known that he'd done wrong? His voice and way of speaking had certainly sounded different, and his actions hardly seemed like the man she'd met earlier, so was this his 'alter' that the report had talked about? Had he finally realised that the alter had left him in a vulnerable situation with nowhere to hide, and the only alternative he had was to flee the scene?

Physically and mentally preparing herself, Fielding rang his doorbell. Hannah stood to the rear but Winters took a stance beside her. The man who opened the door couldn't be more different from the one they'd seen at the hotel.

'Ah,' Burke said recognising her, 'what a pleasant surprise.'

Fielding couldn't be sure if he was being sarcastic or if he genuinely had no recollection of what had just happened. She decided to proceed with extreme caution.

'Do you know who I am?' Paul Winters took one step forward so that the man could see him. At first there didn't appear to be any recognition in his eyes, then realisation sank in.

'Brother!' Burke greeted him with enthusiasm. 'I haven't seen you in person for so long.'

Fielding had difficulty getting her head around the change in personality as she had only seen him less than an hour ago. Was this, then, what having a dual-personality looked like, having another part of the brain taking over and assuming a personality as detached from the physical person as possible? Was that the part of him that they'd witnessed at the pool?

'Come in, come in!' Burke ushered them all into his home. It had an interior as impressive as the exterior. The larger-than-average entrance hall was adorned with Pre-Raphaelite paintings. *Are those originals?* wondered Fielding. Being a bestselling author, the man evidently had money to spend on his material whims.

Leading them into a lounge area, the author indicated that they all be seated. 'Now, what can I help you with?' he asked, seemingly oblivious of all that had taken place within the last hour.

It was DCI Winters who opened up the questioning. 'Do you

remember me getting in touch with you yesterday via your agent?'

Burke looked at him strangely. 'Of course I remember, I'm not gaga yet!' His hearty laugh reverberated around the room.

'And do you know why I contacted you?' Winters continued.

'Yes, I do. You said that you needed to speak to me regarding a case you are working on; something about my researcher wasn't it? Though, I must say,' he continued, 'I hadn't expected to hear from you after all this time, brother.'

Fielding was listening to the conversation with a feeling of dread. If Burke had no inkling of when his personality might change and turn him into his 'alter', which is what she was picking up from the conversation, then the current amicable situation could quickly change. She had no idea what the trigger was, or even if there was one. It could just be a moment's snap and there the other personality was.

But another option came to Fielding's mind. If Burke's alter had committed some of the crimes that he'd written about in his books, then Burke might be aware of his existence. Or had he thought that it had simply come out of his imagination and not from reality? Fielding was no psychologist, but she had done some courses over the years to support a more in-depth knowledge of how a criminal's mind works, and knew that the human brain could be a very fragile piece of equipment under certain circumstances.

'I'm sorry that it's been a while but we've both been leading very busy and different lives,' Winters said.

'True, true,' Burke said. 'Now, what is it that you wish to ask me?'

'Do you remember what happened to our father?'

'Of course,' Burke replied. 'How could I not. Some burglar broke in and he must have disturbed him as the burglar stabbed him. But what has that to do with the case you're on now?'

Winters looked across at Fielding and Hannah in turn. Fielding could see the worried look on his face and she then took over.

'Tell me,' she began. 'How was your father linked to Germany?'

Winters wondered what on earth she was doing, but Fielding knew exactly what she'd asked him.

Burke appeared puzzled by her question. 'Germany?' he repeated. 'My father wasn't linked to Germany. What makes you ask that?'

Fielding was about to continue but noticed his right eye begin to twitch, followed closely by his left. Winters appeared to have noticed it as well as he was about to speak but Fielding raised a hand to stop him.

What happened next happened quickly. Burke's whole personality and voice changed before them. It was as if they were watching a transformation scene from the film *Jekyll and Hyde*, but without all the cinematographic special effects.

'He loved Germany, my father did,' Burke said, in the voice they'd heard by the poolside. 'Even had a German eagle on his belt buckle, the one he used to hit me with when I'd come out from the other one.'

So he was aware of his alter. Had Mr Winters senior known of his son's condition and simply tried to beat it out of him? Fielding felt shocked at the thought of it. Even in the eighties, the idea of multiple personalities was widely acknowledged, but perhaps the man didn't want anyone else to know of it.

'What are you talking about, Father didn't have a German eagle on his belt buckle,' Paul Winters said out loud. 'He'd been in the Royal Air Force; what he had was a buckle with RAF wings on it. I remember it well; I still have it at home as a matter of fact.'

So had all this business with Germany simply come about

due to a mistake? It was a possibility Fielding had to consider. But then why spend years obsessing over it if it had been the cause of all the pain and heartache? And another point to note – which of the two personalities was obsessing about it? Again, fragile minds misconstruing and twisting reality and fiction. Surely, when the young Mark Winters was taken to Stannington Hospital they would have given him the treatment he so desperately needed?

'He had pictures of German aircraft all over the house!' Burke boomed.

'No, that's just not right,' Winters again corrected him. 'They were pictures of RAF aircraft. He was a serving officer; don't you remember?'

Fielding could see the rage build up on Burke's face and could sense that this conversation was heading towards a confrontation, just like the one in the pool area at the hotel.

Only this time Burke didn't have Hannah's gun to grab hold of. Speaking of which, what had happened to the gun? After the sound of it being fired and seeing her partner shot, the only thing on her mind was getting him out of the pool he was sinking deeper into. She looked towards Hannah but she was just staring at the man with a look of horror on her face. When Fielding turned back she saw the cause of her terror. Burke must have somehow kept hold of the weapon and taken it with him when he fled the hotel.

Now he was pointing it directly towards his brother.

In a move that almost defied logic, Winters leapt to his feet and tackled him. It was a brave move. As the two men grappled on the floor, Hannah and Fielding took a few steps backwards. Winters was trying to manoeuvre the gun from his brother's grip. Both had their fingers on the trigger, just like Fielding had witnessed Burke's over Hannah's. She had a very bad feeling that something just as horrific was about to take place.

Then a shot rang out, taking out a vase from a side table. Then another, cracking one of the windowpanes. And finally a third, which left both men lying completely still on the floor. Burke was lying atop of Winters, his body stiff and motionless, and all Hannah and Fielding could do was stand and stare. Seconds felt like hours, but then they saw Winters stir and then manage to force himself free from the weight on top of him then roll his brother over onto his back. There was a bullet hole in the author's chest and a red stain around it.

Neighbours, hearing gunfire, had called the police; and before long a fleet of police cars had formed a line in front of the house, all with their blue lights flashing in unison. A small crowd of curious and concerned people surrounded them.

Fielding went to speak to whoever was in charge, warrant card held up in the air. She knew that a report of gunshots fired would initiate an armed response, and she had no intention of being mistaken for a perpetrator. Hannah would have to explain how she'd come to have a gun in the first place. What had she been thinking bringing one? And where had she got it from?

The officer in charge let Fielding tell him what had happened, took a quick look around the premises and arranged for the body to be removed from the house.

Then he took Fielding, Winters and Hannah into another room to discuss the circumstances that had led up to Burke's death. The man looked shocked as the tale unfolded. As Fielding had predicted, the main cause of concern was Hannah's weapon, or more specifically, why she'd brought it along with her in the first place. The retired detective would have a lot to answer for: her weapon had caused one man's death and wounded another...

At that moment it suddenly hit Fielding that Burton might have succumbed to one of its bullets as well.

45

'Where's Joe?' Christine Fielding asked, looking beyond her daughter but realising that she was on her own. Reaching for the light switch by the front door she turned it on, and it was then she saw the blood on her daughter's face and clothing.

'Sally, what's happened?' she exclaimed, horrified by the sight. Her daughter looked a mess, and her clothes also looked damp as if she'd been in water.

Sally could hardly speak but managed to say, 'It's Joe, he's been shot.'

'Is he okay?' Mrs Fielding was almost afraid to ask. It was a situation all police officers' families feared, being told that there'd been a shooting or that their loved one had been injured, or worse, in the line of duty.

'I've just called the hospital and he's in surgery. That's all they can tell me right now.'

'Oh, Sally, no. No! Do you want to talk about it, or do you just want me to leave you alone for a while? Whatever you want, I'm happy to do it.'

It was then that Sally realised that this was the moment she would have to tell her mother everything about her father's death. No putting it off now, as it needed to be done. What they'd been led to believe for all those years was now known to be a lie, and her mother deserved to know the facts as well. Sally knew and now it was her mother's turn to also know.

Plucking up the courage she said, 'Let's have a cup of tea, shall we, Mum? There's something I need to tell you.'

46

The funeral had taken place at 11am on a Thursday. It had been a bitterly cold day, with grey clouds hanging low in the sky.

Everyone he worked with turned up; after all, he had been a very popular man, loved by all.

Fielding hadn't thought that she could face the funeral of the man she loved so deeply, but she did. She had forced herself to do it by clearing her mind of everything except the notion of getting through the day. It was what she had always been good at, taking herself out of a situation when it was far too painful for her to bear.

It had been, she realised later, an unhealthy tactic, and dreams about that funeral still haunted her fifteen years later. But this time, she found herself focussing not on the grief that had consumed her teenage self, but the colleagues gathered there. And everything slipped into place. *So that's why he had looked so familiar – that's why they'd both looked so familiar.*

The first time she had worked with Paul Winters she knew that there was something about him, and the same with Jonas Burke when she'd seen his cardboard cut-out standee in the window of the bookstore in Manchester. They did look so much alike now that she knew they were brothers.

Hannah had been at the funeral, too, with her husband.

It was right then that she woke up. It wasn't so much a nightmare as a dream of remembrance. Her father had been laid to rest, and Paul Winters had attended the funeral. Now she remembered.

47

His eyes were blurry at first, but he knew for a fact that he was no longer sinking to the bottom of a swimming pool. He felt disorientated; the light around him was so bright that he couldn't focus clearly on anything. Then a familiar voice.

'Ah, there you are!' DCI Elizabeth Ambleton got up from her chair and stood by the side of the bed. 'We thought that we'd lost you, Joe,' she said, looking down at him.

He tried to move but felt a soreness in the right side which made him wince.

'Keep still, you'll have those stitches pulled out if you try to move too much,' Ambleton told him.

Since when did she become a doctor? Burton thought. As he began to focus enough to get his bearings, he found that he was in a hospital room. A cannula in the vein of his left arm was pumping in some kind of clear liquid, and a machine off to his right was monitoring his blood pressure and pulse rate.

'What on earth happened?' he managed to say with a croaky voice.

'What do you remember?' Ambleton asked.

'Well ... Fielding and I were in a hotel in Boldon, and I think I heard a shot from somewhere...'

'That's exactly what happened–'

'Wait,' Burton cut in, 'what are you doing up in the north east?'

'I'm not in the north east, nor are you,' she told him, 'you're now in Manchester; we had you brought back here after you were shot.'

'I've been shot?' Burton seemed surprised to hear that little piece of news. So that's what the pain in his side was. He remembered the sound of a gun then ... what ... water? Yes, he remembered going into the pool, the feeling that he was sinking, and then...

'Did somebody jump in the pool?' he asked.

Ambleton nodded. 'Who do you think jumped in?' she asked him with a smile.

'Fielding?'

'Yes, she did.'

Burton put his head back onto the pillow. His throat was sore and talking was becoming more difficult. Sensing his discomfort, Ambleton said that she would leave him in peace promising to let the team know that he was now awake.

'Are you feeling up to visitors? Because I know of a few people who have been waiting to come in to see you.'

He nodded, feeling very weary.

She put a friendly hand on his shoulder. 'I'll let the nurses know you're awake. They may even offer you something for that pain. I'd take it if I were you.'

'I will,' he managed to say to her before she left. Now on his own, he had time to try to remember exactly what had happened that had brought him to a hospital bed.

Over the course of the day his memory of events came back

to him all too clearly. He could see himself sinking slowly to the bottom of the pool, unable to either move his arms or kick his legs. His body had seemed to have accepted that this was the end of his journey through life. Then he'd seen a figure jumping in, but that had only been for a brief moment as blackness closed in.

The doctor came in, and talked to him about his injuries. Burton wasn't entirely sure what his gallbladder was or indeed its function, but apparently he no longer owned one. 'Life will go on as normal,' the doctor assured him. 'Just a few dietary adjustments needed.'

So Burton was happy to still be in the land of the living.

Fielding came in to see him that evening, by which time he was starting to feel somewhat better although very sleepy, and that could be in some part down the good and regular supply of pain relief medication.

Fielding was surprised to see him looking so well, considering all that he'd been through.

'I thought that you'd want to stay back up in the north east?' was the first thing that he spouted forth on seeing her.

She laughed. 'Oh, why's that?' she asked, wondering where this line of thinking had come from.

'Back to the land of your roots and all that.'

'No, no. Manchester is my home now, you know that.'

'But with you reconnecting with your family, I thought that you'd want to stay?'

'Are you trying to get rid of me or something?' She laughed again, wondering if it was the pain medication that was talking rather than him.

'Of course not!'

'I hear that you're missing an organ?' she asked him, concerned about the removal of his gallbladder.

'Yes, I heard that too. But I'm sure that it will grow back.'

'Oh dear, just how much medication are they giving you?' She looked over at the drip going into his arm, which was sending a steady feed into his vein via the cannula. 'They don't grow back, you know.'

'Don't they?' He yawned, before he laid his head back on the pillow and closed his eyes.

Fielding took that as her cue to leave. She was overjoyed that he'd survived his ordeal, despite the loss of an organ, and that he'd be fit to return to work in a couple of months. In the meantime she and DC Jack Summers had again been partnered, just as they had during their undercover work in the homeless man case. She knew that Summers had had potential then and was happy to see that potential being recognised. His temporary promotion would stand him in good stead for the future as he'd already stepped up and filled the role perfectly.

48

After a couple of days convalescing Joe Burton began to feel a whole lot better.

He vaguely remembered DCI Ambleton and Sally Fielding coming in to see him, but trying to remember what they'd said, and what he'd said to them in return, was like trying to manoeuvre his way through a thick blanket of fog. He accepted that this was most likely down to his pain medication, but he sincerely hoped that he hadn't said or done anything amiss during that time of blankness.

He'd visited people in hospital following operations and they'd all been vague at best, and trying to have a coherent conversation with them was nigh-on impossible. Understandable when they'd been given a general anaesthetic, which essentially puts the body into an induced coma.

He knew that eliminating anaesthetic drugs from the system could take up to a week for some people, so he just hoped that he hadn't made a fool of himself whilst in this relaxed and forgetful state. He gave up trying to remember; his memory would come back when it did, naturally.

However, the first thing that he remembered was what Elizabeth Ambleton had told him about his partner. Sally Fielding, the person he knew to be a far-from-accomplished swimmer, had jumped in the swimming pool when he'd been shot and dragged him to the side of the pool, essentially saving his life.

Then if that wasn't enough, Paul Winters had performed CPR on him until the paramedics arrived. That was something he couldn't forget, and would be eternally grateful for. He could have easily died that night but for his quick-thinking colleagues at the scene and, of course, the actions of the emergency services.

Over the next few days his memory returned completely and he was now anxious to know what had happened after he'd been shot. During that time, and acting on the advice of Burton's attending doctor, DCI Ambleton had instructed her team to avoid mentioning anything to do with the case when they visited him. Light conversation only. The medical staff thought it best to let his memory return naturally until he could cope, and thereby remove any unnecessary stress for him while he was recuperating.

One of his first visitors after the fog had lifted was DCI Paul Winters, who had travelled down to Manchester specifically to see how he was. Winters had been in direct communication with both DS Fielding and DCI Ambleton for the duration of Burton's hospitalisation and, like them, was waiting patiently to fill him in on all that had occurred after his shooting. And there was so much to tell him.

Burton was surprised, yet delighted to see the detective from Northumbria Police, and was grateful for the opportunity to thank the man in person. He now had pangs of guilt for having doubted him throughout, especially as he now knew that Winters had played no part in it. But Burton also knew what working a case involved – suspect everyone, especially when the signs point to a person's involvement, no matter who or what they are. Winters would doubtlessly agree and have done the same in his position.

With their initial formalities over, Winters got down to the business of filling in the blanks for him.

'The forensics team went over Burke's house in Hexham with a fine-tooth comb and they were able to provide me with further insight into the man's past.'

Winters was very successfully holding back any emotion but Burton could see the pain in his eyes when he talked about his sibling. He referred to him as 'Burke' or 'the man'. Was he trying to depersonalise the situation by not referring to him as 'my brother' or 'Mark'?

Burton knew from Winters's personnel file that both he and his mother had disowned Mark Winters, the man who would become Jonas Burke, following the death of the family's patriarch. But it must have still been a sensitive issue for Paul Winters and rightly so. How many people could say that they had a brother who had murdered their father? And how many of them would actually talk about it openly?

But the detective seemed to collect himself, and said, 'Now here's a puzzle for you, Burton. Do you remember DS Koder, the non-existent officer who signed off all those cases?'

Burton nodded. How could he not? It was one of the main things they'd found that alerted them to something being way off kilter.

'Well, forensics found documents – copies of confidential case notes which he'd used in his novels and not the amended ones signed by a fictitious DS Koder. And that was the first of many German connections they came across. As we then discovered, *Köder* is German for bait, and perhaps it was Burke's whimsical way of taunting anyone who ever happened to come across his activities.'

Burton shook his head. Word play was not his idea of a good joke. 'And was it him altering the police database?'

Winters looked serious. 'The truth is, we don't know. It seems that he studied computer science to degree level, before moving into journalism, and might have had enough knowledge to gain access into a police database in order to change it. Or if it wasn't him, then the chances were that he knew of someone who could. Money wouldn't be a problem for him, so he could certainly afford to pay a hacker to do it.'

'And now tell me about the letter W,' said Burton, remembering the other thing that had puzzled him.

'The letter W or, as Fielding discovered,' said Winters, steepling his fingers, 'the two letter Vs, stood for *vernichten* and *verderben*. The first being "exterminate" and the second "killed". So it appeared that the victims were chosen for death, and then marked off as being killed when they had been. All clearly marked in his personal notes. Jonas Burke hated all things German, based on an odd misunderstanding all those years ago. He had mistaken my father's love of the RAF for a love for Germany.'

Burton admired the way Winters could stand back and view everything from an objective perspective. Yes, it was hurting him, Burton could see that in his whole body language. After all, Burke was his blood brother, but he was also a stranger to him as he hadn't seen him since the day he was carried off in an ambulance to Stannington Hospital.

'You see,' Burton voiced his thoughts when Winters had finished talking, 'that's what I don't understand. If Burke hated all things German for all the wrong reasons, then why did he persist with the use of it? It doesn't make any kind of sense.'

'I know, and I really can't give you a definitive answer. I've spoken to our psychology expert about exactly that and she seemed to think that, apart from the dissociative identity disorder, Burke could have also been experiencing hallucinations and seeing something that wasn't there. I think it seems to be a logical conclusion and perhaps the only answer, the only one I can think of anyway. I suppose somewhere in his fractured mind the other self, or selves, caused mental confusion way beyond anything any non-sufferer can comprehend.'

'We'll never know for sure then?'

Winters shook his head. 'No, we certainly won't.'

'So from what forensics also discovered it looks like Burke – or rather his alter – was instrumental in deaths in the twenty-five cases you'd pulled out as being identical to those featured in his books. Perhaps he thought that he'd just imagined it and written down what his mind had conjured up, but it looked like his alter had taken over and shown him first-hand just what death looked and felt like. He then went on to describe in great detail in his books the manner in which the victims had died. Other handwritten documents found seemed to indicate that two clear personalities existed as alters – the one who had no compunction about murdering anyone, and another who appeared to be adept in research and information skills. Had he lived, the psychiatrists would have had a field day trying to figure out if Burke knew what he was doing or not. But as he potentially had the knowledge to either hack or get somebody else to get into database files and change them, then the chances were that he did know or, at the very least, be aware that someone or something was telling him to do it. The complexities of the human mind, eh?'

'So what about all the other suspects?' Burton was keen to know if anyone else they'd questioned had been involved.

'They're all innocent parties,' Winters confirmed, 'every last one of them, even Mendelson with his German name, which, as it turned out, was merely a coincidence. However, I can't imagine how Burke coped with Mendelson's wife being his number one super-fan, under the circumstances. I believe he even visited her at one point to see the collection she had on him. He must have done it with gritted teeth. Probably the only reason he went through with it was for the publicity, as I gather the article was featured in a lot of the daily papers.'

'But what about the two tech people who knocked me out and also menaced Doris Mendelson?' wondered Burton.

Winters grimaced. 'They remain unknown, but we think that they were hired by Burke to carry out his subterfuge locally. Their names and identities haven't been discovered in his documents, and the CCTV at police HQ was unmatchable with any persons held on record. So I'm afraid we've stopped looking.'

'Unbelievable,' Burton muttered. Then he thought that he had to say something regarding his suspicions about Winters. 'Look–' he began, not making eye contact.

But Winters must have anticipated where the conversation was heading. 'There's really no need,' he began as Burton finally looked at him, 'I know what you're going to say and I would have done the same under the circumstances. Obviously, I didn't make the whole thing regarding my estranged brother public knowledge, didn't really want to, if truth be told, I mean who would? But the incident is in my service records, as I'm sure you are aware.'

Burton felt his face flush, and it wasn't through the warmth of the room he was in, but Winters continued to put him at ease. 'Always seek out the facts, right?'

Again, Burton nodded. 'So what about Hannah; what's happened to her?'

'Now that's a different story,' Winters told him. And this time he made no attempt to conceal his sorrow and regret.

49

Four days after Jonas Burke's demise there had been an enquiry into the whole case and Hannah hadn't escaped unscathed.

She was charged with possession of a dangerous weapon. But DCI Paul Winters had spoken up on her behalf in front of the judge, and what could have had very serious consequences for her, including prison time, resulted in a suspended sentence with probation.

She promised herself that she would never read a crime novel again. Winters had not been convicted of any wrongdoing as he'd tried to disarm his brother when he produced the gun.

However, that wasn't the end of Hannah's misery or her shame. The story was front page news in the local and national newspapers, which had far-reaching repercussions, though she was spared a spell in prison.

While in police custody prior to her appearance in front of a judge, she had been visited by her daughter, Amy, who was far from happy with her mother's actions and made her fully aware of it.

'What on earth were you thinking, Mum?' Hannah's distraught and red-eyed daughter had asked her when the two of them were seated together in an interview room. It was hardly a private meeting between mother and daughter as a female constable stood nearby throughout. 'Do you realise how bad all this is – for me and Millie as much as you. I'm a respected teacher, for heaven's sake and you ... well, you're a retired police officer who should have known better. What was even going through your mind? I didn't even know that you'd kept that old pistol of Granddad's. I thought that you'd handed it in when they had a gun amnesty. So why, oh why did you decide to take it with you?'

Tears began to form in her eyes as Hannah finally plucked up the courage to even look at her daughter's face. 'If you can just give me a chance to explain–'

'Explain! How can there be anything to explain?'

'Amy, please. Let me tell you what happened.'

Frustrated and annoyed, Amy sat back in the chair and folded her arms across her chest, her eyes never leaving her mother's face, waiting for a credible explanation to come forth. She had exhausted everything she could possibly say to her mother. Embarrassed to the point of shame, she'd taken time away from work and had removed Millie from school as she couldn't face any backlash regarding her mother's crime. And that was what she saw it as, a crime. Hannah knew that, she knew her own flesh and blood so well, but she was determined to have her say and to tell her daughter the reasons for her doing what she did.

'I wanted to avenge my partner's death,' she began.

'What, by taking the gun and shooting the person you thought might have been responsible?' Amy asked incredulously, her eyebrows raised so high they almost disappeared beneath her fringe.

'No, no, of course not,' Hannah shook her head. This was going to take a lot of explaining, she knew that, but deep down she hoped that Amy could understand the reasoning behind her decision. 'When I decided to take it along to the meeting with Burke I never in my wildest dreams imagined that he would get his hands on it. It was just for appearance's sake. I checked it before I took it; the safety catch was on, so I knew that if I brought it out it would be safe for me to do so. So when Burke managed to get it off me and take the safety catch off, and it had actually fired and shot Joe Burton, I was horrified.'

'Oh, Mum!' Amy began in less aggressive tones.

Surely she couldn't have thought that I took it there to actually shoot anybody? Hannah asked herself, but at least her daughter's tone had changed, which gave her hope that she might eventually come to understand her actions.

'Then, of course, nobody realised that he had taken it away with him when he fled the scene; everybody was all far too concerned about Joe Burton's wellbeing, me included.'

'So how come you were even there in the first place? Weren't you just supposed to be working with them in an advisory capacity?'

'I wanted to know what William had shouted out to me before he died. I always thought it was relevant but I just couldn't hear what he was saying. I felt he must have known who the killer was. Also, I felt frustrated by how long the investigation was taking. I know that I should have left it all to Joe Burton and Sally Fielding: they're both professionals and were doing a very good job. There should be more like them in the force in my opinion—'

'Mum,' Amy cut in, realising that her mother was digressing.

'But I felt they should have brought Burke into the station, rather than just telephoning him or going off to Sheffield to see him in a bookstore. The man was hiding something, I knew it from the start. Don't ask me how I knew, I just did,' she said when she saw her daughter looking at her with something now akin to pity.

'I felt they were shutting me out. After all, William Fielding was my partner – and my friend. He was Sally Fielding's father, so I know it was personal for her as well. I couldn't figure out why they were avoiding the obvious – and that was to bring him in. Plus, I felt that you and Millie were being targeted too, with the parcel addressed to me but delivered to your address. It had to be something to do with the case: it couldn't not be.'

'So how did you end up meeting Burke?' Amy now wanted to hear the story out, to understand why things had escalated.

'I thought that Burton's mistrust of Paul was paranoia. I've known Paul for many years and I knew that he couldn't have been involved in all of this. Of course, when I found out that Burton had gone into the personnel files and discovered that Burke was Paul's brother I was both shocked and annoyed. Annoyed that Burton had searched his file, and also shocked and annoyed that Paul had never discussed this with me.'

'But that's something Paul Winters probably wouldn't have wanted to talk about with anybody, including his work colleagues.'

Hannah knew that her daughter was correct, she could see that, but she had felt such anger at the time. And for that reason she had gone up to his office to confront him about it.

'I insisted Paul contact his brother and set up a meeting with him. Paul told me that he hadn't seen his brother since childhood and wasn't aware of his name change or fame. Although this initially seemed incredible, there was little evidence to doubt him on that, especially as I now knew from his file that ties had been cut when their father had been murdered. Families had disowned one another for far less. But I could see all the facts in the case pointing towards Burke playing a pivotal role. I just had to speak to him about the one thing that had been bothering me in all this. Of course I wanted to know how he got access to the information in the files; but what I needed to know more than anything was had he killed my partner. It was something I had to know first-hand.'

'But you shouldn't have done it alone, not without the two detectives.'

'I know, Amy, but by now I don't think I was being logical. Paul said he didn't want to see his brother again, but I argued him round. So he contacted Burke's agent saying that Northumbria Police needed to speak to him as a matter of some urgency. Burke had chosen the location which, ironically, was exactly where William Fielding had died. That, in itself, made Winters wonder how far his estranged brother was involved in all this. At this stage none of us knew anything of his brother's alternate personalities, but Paul had always believed him to be responsible for their father's death all those years ago.'

'And did Burke confess?'

'At first he claimed ignorance of everything. But perhaps it was the setting and the memory of what had occurred there in the past that brought out one of his alters. When I produced the gun from my bag, just as a visual threat you understand, it sent Burke into a metamorphosis in which an alter stated that yes, he had done all those things, including tasering William.'

'And why were those two other detectives even there?'

'They followed us. I had no idea that they had. But when Joe Burton confronted Burke he overcame me and put his finger over mine on the trigger. I mistakenly let Burton know that the safety catch was on, which also informed Burke. Somehow he managed to loosen his grip on me long enough to take it off and pressed so hard on the trigger that it went off.'

'Well that puts a different light on things,' Amy eventually said, 'but it still doesn't excuse you taking the weapon there in the first place.'

'I know, I know,' Hannah hung her head again. 'I know I should have made different decisions, but at the time it seemed like the only thing to do.'

50

Well into the second month of the new year, Joe Burton returned to work. During that time Sally Fielding had paid numerous visits to him and had kept him updated on all that was happening, so that when the time came he'd have the heads-up on all that was going on.

She'd even, to his embarrassment, arranged for 'welcome home' bunting to be looped around the squad room and in his office, as well as several dozen balloons.

At the end of his first week back, late on Friday afternoon, DCI Ambleton called him up to her office. He knew that she would be conducting a back-to-work interview with him, but what he didn't know was that she also had some very important news to impart to him.

'Sit down, Joe.' She'd immediately ushered him into the seat across the desk from her. 'How are you feeling?'

'I'm doing all right, thanks, boss,' he said sitting down cautiously. Although he was fit to work, his recovering wound from the removal of his gallbladder still ached from time to time. The scar was looking good and healing very well according to his consultant, but he was still erring on the side of caution when it came to over-exertion. At least this was better than having to use a stick, as he had to do in the first few weeks post-surgery. He smiled to himself as he remembered what Fielding had said to him when she'd seen him hobbling around his house – 'You're walking like an old man, Burton.' He'd felt like an old man at the time but, thankfully, that was all behind him now. However, he still took it easy just in case.

'Good, good,' she smiled. Like everybody else on the team she had been on tenterhooks waiting to hear how his surgery had gone on the day of his shooting. And, again like everybody else, had been overjoyed to hear the good news that he was going to pull through. She couldn't imagine a world without Joe Burton in it. He was one of, if not the best of all the police officers she'd had the pleasure to know and work with over the years. Apart from her own partnership with him before her appointment to DCI, his and Fielding's was now one of the most admired pairings on the force. They were both strong, solid upstanding officers, the kind others aim to be, and they were still relatively young to attain that sort of admiration from their colleagues. Usually it was the older, more established officers who claimed that prize, which said a great deal for Burton and Fielding's charisma and dedication. Like many others, she thought that the two should perhaps be partnered in another way, outside of work. Perhaps what she was to say to him now might have some bearing on that.

'Well I have some news that I would like you to be the first to hear,' Ambleton continued, and Burton raised a quizzical eyebrow.

'I've decided to retire in the summer,' she continued. Burton was thrilled for her, but hoped that she was going for all the right reasons. She had always confided in him regarding what was going on with her son, Charlie, and hoped that her decision to retire hadn't been based on the need to be at home and give him extra support.

'Alistair and I have decided to retire simultaneously. As you know, I wasn't due to go for another eighteen months or so, but with Charlie now back on track, and good support at hand if he should need it again, we decided that we can now do all the things that we wanted to do together before we get any older.'

She laughed and he could tell that she was relieved that her son had improved so much. She hadn't mentioned him a great deal over the last few months, and he was a little afraid to ask in case her response about his condition wasn't good. It was great to see that the weight had been lifted from her as he knew how much anguish she had suffered over Charlie's welfare.

'That's great, boss. Congratulations.'

'Thank you. Which means,' she continued, 'that the powers-that-be will be looking for a new DCI, and I will be putting your name forward for the promotion.'

'What?' was all Burton could say. Of course, he'd hoped to reach that rank one day, five or ten years' time maybe, but this was an opportunity he hadn't expected to come around so soon.

'Are you up for it?' Ambleton asked, beaming broadly at him. There was only one person in her mind who she'd want to fill her shoes and he was sitting right opposite her now.

'Yes,' he managed to get out. He could feel himself shaking beneath his usually strong exterior. 'Wow,' he said, putting a hand up to his now-damp forehead.

Ambleton laughed as she rose from her seat and held out a hand to him. 'I know I said I put you forward, but I have it on very good authority that the job is as good as yours if you want it.'

'I don't know what to say,' he told her, taking her outstretched hand and shaking it a little more vigorously than perhaps he intended to before letting it go.

'Just one thing,' Ambleton added. 'Don't tell the team at the minute; let it be a surprise for them when it's officially announced.'

'Okay. Not even Fielding?'

'Yes you can tell Sally but ask her to keep it to herself. I knew that you'd want to tell her. Who knows, perhaps your promotion will mean that you two can now have a more personal relationship.'

'I'm sorry?'

'Come on, Joe,' she smiled. 'We both know you two should be a little more than just partners at work.'

Burton looked shocked. It was true that he'd always felt a great deal for his partner and under different circumstances they may have already been together as a couple, but it was not something he believed to be common knowledge.

'I–' he began, but Ambleton spared him the embarrassment.

'Go on, off you go.' She gave him a friendly slap on the back.

As he was going down in the lift Burton mulled over what he'd just been told. Yes, the promotion would be fantastic, but it was what his boss had implied about his relationship with Sally that was uppermost in his thoughts.

Was she trying to say that if they were not partnered it wouldn't be frowned upon for them to engage in a relationship outside of work? Had he heard that part correctly? She had taken him completely by surprise by even mentioning any possibility of a romantic liaison between them, but now that she'd mentioned it, could it indeed be a possibility after all this time? The idea excited him. In the seven years that they'd been partnered together of course he'd thought about her in a non-work way, but knew the rules and regulations as well as any other serving police officer. However, this threw a different light on things.

As he entered the squad room he stopped beside Fielding's desk and asked if she could come into his office with him. She locked her computer, got up from her seat and followed him in, closing the door behind her.

'I've got a bit of news,' he told her after they'd both sat down. He outlined what Ambleton had told him.

'Many congratulations, Joe!' She was thrilled by the news, yet at the same time she realised that if that was the case then they'd no longer be partnered together, and for that reason had conflicting thoughts.

'I was wondering...' he began. Here it was, he was finally going to ask her. He'd started so he had no other option than to finish the question. '...if you'd like to go out for a drink tonight to celebrate?'

'Oooooh, yes, of course, that would be a great night out for all the team.'

'Ambleton said not to tell anybody, though, not until the official announcement comes through.'

Sally understood. 'No, of course not. My lips are sealed.' She made the motion of drawing an imaginary zip across her mouth.

Then realisation set in. 'You mean just the two of us?'

'Yes. Would that be a problem?'

She looked at him; he looked so nervous sitting there asking her out. Wait ... what? 'Joe, are you asking me out on a date?'

'Well, if you want to call it that then, yes.'

'But what about protocol?'

'Ambleton seems to think that would be okay, seeing that we wouldn't be directly working together.'

'What? You discussed this with Ambleton?'

'More like she discussed it with me. She seemed to imply that the whole world and his wife thinks we should be together!'

He made it sound jokey as if he was perfectly at ease with discussing this with her – but that couldn't have been further from the truth.

Her silence worried him, and her expression gave nothing away whatsoever. It was as if she, too, was as shocked as he had been up in the boss's office.

'Well?' he asked after a while, as frightened as a spotty-faced schoolboy asking the school's most beautiful girl out on a date. 'What do you say?'

'Yes,' she replied, smiling broadly. 'I've been waiting seven years for you to ask me that question, Joe Burton!'

THE END

ACKNOWLEDGEMENTS

I'd like to thank everyone at Bloodhound Books for their continued help and support.

Special thanks go to my editor, Clare Law, and to Fred Freeman, Betsy Reavley, Heather Fitt, Tara Lyons and Sumaira Wilson for all the hard work they do behind the scenes.

Thank you, Paul Pilkington, for acknowledging me in your latest book. I have enjoyed reading your books over the years, and you have inspired me to take my own writing journey more seriously.

If you have enjoyed reading this please consider leaving a review on Amazon. It need only be a few words and it means a lot to authors to get feedback from their readers.

Printed in Great Britain
by Amazon